THE MORTICIAN'S DAUGHTER

By the Author

London Undone

The Mortician's Daughter

THE MORTICIAN'S DAUGHTER

by
Nan Higgins

2020

ISBN 13: 978-1-63555-594-3

This Trade Paperback Original Is Published By
Bold Strokes Books, Inc.
P.O. Box 249
Valley Falls, NY 12185

First Edition: April 2020

CREDITS
EDITORS: Barbara Ann Wright and Stacia Seaman
Production Design: Stacia Seaman
Cover Design by Tammy Seidick

Acknowledgments

This book is a result of unending support from my fiancée, Misti Simmons, and my sons, Ben and Edison. Without their constant belief in me, and their generosity in creating time and space for me to write, none of this would have been possible.

My two great writing buddies and best sounding boards are Octavia Reese and fellow BSB author Annie McDonald. I can always count on them for advice and clarity.

Finally, I must thank everyone at Bold Strokes Books for their constant care and guidance. I'm especially grateful to my editor, Barbara Ann Wright, for all of her wisdom and skilled guidance.

For Gabe and Jason, and a lifetime of our legendary bad movie nights.

CHAPTER ONE

I was trying to make the best of my birthday party.

What I wanted was a chill night out with a few friends to celebrate turning twenty-two. Macy had organized a party where we'd meet some other friends from high school at Dewey's Pizza and end up at the fire pit in her backyard, probably with beer and stuff to make s'mores.

What I got was a formal dinner at an upscale restaurant with my parents. I'd talked Macy into coming since I couldn't get out of it. I could barely stifle a giggle every time I looked at her.

Macy didn't wear dresses. Even in high school, when we had a choir concert and the standard uniform was a white blouse and black skirt, Macy always wore pants instead. But when she came home from college to celebrate my birthday, she hadn't foreseen having to bring dress pants. She'd had to borrow a dress from her mom to adhere to the dress code at Mitchell's Steak House. Seeing her cross and uncross her legs beneath the burgundy floral-print skirt made me grab my napkin and press it to my mouth to cover a snicker, but not before she heard me. My laugh turned to a grimace when she gave me a sharp kick under the table.

"Serves you right," she muttered.

"What's that, dear?" my mother asked.

"This steak is just right," Macy said.

My mom lifted her glass and smiled broadly. "So glad you're enjoying it."

"Shall we have a toast?" My dad raised his glass too and peered around the table until Macy and I held our glasses in the air. "To Aria, my amazing and talented daughter. I can't believe you're twenty-two already. Anyone who denies how quickly time passes surely must not be a parent. I'm so proud of the young lady you're becoming. You have the voice of an angel and the heart of a lion. Happy birthday."

"Cheers," my mom said. The four of us tapped our glasses, my parents' filled with champagne, mine a strawberry daiquiri, and Macy's a rum and Coke.

"Thank you," I said. This was nice. It wasn't what I had in mind, but it was nice of my parents, and Macy had rearranged our plans so the pizza and bonfire could still happen tomorrow night. It was right that I be with my parents on my actual birthday. I knew they'd missed having these occasions when I was in New York in school. "Thank you all so much."

"This seems like a good time to do presents," my mom said.

"Now, Joanna?" My dad arched an eyebrow.

"I can't wait anymore," she said, laughing. "Do you want to go first?"

He stroked his beard and gazed toward the ceiling, nodding in a way that was meant to seem absentminded but was clearly choreographed. Macy elbowed me and giggled. She could never get over my parents' theatrics.

"I think I will." He rubbed his hands together and grinned at my mom. "You won't have the best gift this year, I guarantee it."

My mom swept her arm out across the table, smiling back. "Let's see what you've got."

Dad reached into his jacket pocket and pulled out a navy-blue box the size of his palm. "The best gifts come in small packages, my dear. Everyone knows that." He set the box in front of me, still smiling.

I heard the jingle of keys inside. It couldn't be. I opened it and found the keys to a Honda Civic. "*A car!*" I screeched.

"You deserve it, sweetheart," Dad said. "You work so hard. And it's a used car, nothing fancy, but it's safe and reliable, and it'll get you where you're going. As long as you pay for the insurance, you'll be all set."

I'd had an old beater in high school, but when I got my acceptance letter to NYU, I'd sold it for cash to buy books, knowing I'd never drive when I was there. "I don't know what to say," I said, the box shaking in my hands. "Thank you. I didn't expect this."

"You're welcome."

"Well," my mom said, a stage frown pulling her dark eyebrows together, "it seems you have won this year, Nathan. I'm afraid I can't compete with a new car or even a used one." She pulled an envelope out of her purse. "Maybe I shouldn't even bother giving you my gift."

I set the box on the table and held my hands out. "What is it, what it is, what is it?"

Mom set the envelope gently in my hands; she had tears in her eyes. I took a deep breath and, hands still shaking, opened the envelope. A piece of stationery from MoodWave Media fell onto the table. I looked up at my parents. My dad smiled broadly and put his arm around my mom, who now had a few tears on her cheeks. I picked up the letter from Angela Osborn, the producer to whom I'd sent my demo.

I'd gotten phone calls and emails from Ms. Osborn's office for quite some time now. She had come to some of my performances at NYU and had already attended a few of my gigs around the city. Things had seemed to be going well, but a couple weeks had gone by, and I hadn't heard anything else from her. This letter confirmed Angela would be at my big performance next month at the Vern Riffe Center. If all went well, I'd be moving out to LA this summer to try to get started on my music career.

"How long have you known?" I asked.

"It came yesterday, but we wanted to surprise you for your birthday," Mom said, dabbing at a tear with her napkin.

I was lucky I wasn't required to sing in that moment. My throat was thick—almost chokingly so—with the combination of gratitude and disbelief that bubbled inside me. The dream that had consumed my life since my earliest memories was on the edge of coming true, and it felt so unreal. Images flooded my vision of all the times I'd stayed up late practicing, forgoing sleep, parties, and dates in favor of learning new music for a gig or working on getting a song perfect or just improving my technique. Every moment had been a step toward what would soon be my dream realized, and it seemed both perfectly right and completely impossible. I tried to swallow, which only seemed to enlarge the lump in my throat.

"Congratulations, Aria." Macy leaned in to give me a hug, and I squeezed her hard. "You earned this."

"Thank you," I said. I hugged the letter to my chest.

CHAPTER TWO

Macy leaned against the counter in the bathroom at Mitchell's and bared her teeth into the mirror, looking for food. When she didn't find any, she closed her mouth and tucked some of her dreadlocks back into the high ponytail she wore whenever she dressed up.

"It's going to be weird this summer without you." She picked up my purse and rummaged through it. She grabbed the mauve lipstick I always carry because it's one of the few shades that looks great on both of us—with my nearly Casper-like skin and hers the hue of brown autumn leaves, it's difficult to find a lip color that suits us both—and began applying it.

It would be the first time she and I had spent more than a day or two apart since we met in kindergarten. Miss Caldecott prepared us for the rest of our elementary school careers by seating us alphabetically by last name. We weren't always in the same class, but when we were, Macy Holmes sat next to Aria Jasper. We'd been inseparable since day one. We hadn't even been apart for college since both of us had dreamed of going to NYU since we were little.

"I'll be back and forth." I looked in the mirror and ran my fingers through my own dark, shoulder length hair. "You know I'll always visit."

Macy pouted. "It's not the same. Don't get me wrong, I'm

happy for you. I know how hard you worked for this. But there's going to be literally nothing for me to do here when you're gone."

I snorted. "There's going to be plenty to do. This is Columbus, Ohio, not Siberia."

"Compared to Los Angeles, this is BFE." She dropped the lipstick back in my purse with a clatter. "You done primping?"

"Yeah. You?"

"Yep."

We stepped out of the bathroom, arms linked, and walked back to our table. The opulent bar twinkled on the opposite end of the restaurant. I glanced over and stopped. My dad was at the bar talking to a distraught older man. Or rather, the man was talking while my dad glanced around. There had only been a handful of times when I'd seen my dad look anything other than self-assured and steady. Now he appeared nervous and jittery. He said something to the man, who became more animated, hands gesturing wildly.

"Oh my God," I breathed.

"Um, is your dad okay?" Macy asked.

"I don't know. Should we check on him?"

"My mom says not to interrupt someone who's talking to themselves. She thinks it's rude."

I jerked around to face her. "What? My dad's not talking to himself."

Macy looked from me to my dad. "I was just joking. I mean, I'm sure he has a Bluetooth thing in his ear or something."

Mouth agape, I turned back to the bar. The stranger had a hand on my dad's shoulder and was standing inches from his face. Even so, my dad was looking directly at me, and he'd gone very pale.

CHAPTER THREE

Macy and I were in our sleeping bags in the basement, a bowl of popcorn between us. We were watching an old B-horror movie from my parents' collection: *Killer Klowns from Outer Space*. We had the volume turned down to almost nothing so we could voice our own version of the dialogue. It had been a slumber party tradition since we were little.

I'd been turning over the events at the restaurant in my mind, trying to make sense of what had happened. Maybe Macy hadn't seen the man speaking to my father? But how could that be? He had been fussing and making quite a scene…except that wasn't quite true. I'd been trying to put my finger on what had been strange about the situation, aside from the fact that Macy couldn't see someone who had been only a few feet away from her. I realized that even though the older man had been gesturing wildly and seemed quite agitated, nobody had been paying attention to him. Even my father had appeared to be pretending not to see him. But why?

A soft knock at the door interrupted our dialogue riff. "Come in," I said.

Dad stuck his head in. "How's it going, girls?"

"Good," we said in unison.

"Excellent. Ah, Aria, can you come help me with something for a minute?"

"Sure. Let's pause this."

Macy pushed a button on the remote, and the killer klown froze in his tracks. I followed my dad upstairs to the kitchen where my mom sat at the table, her eyes red and puffy, and her face shiny with tears. I sat in the chair next to her, scooting close so I could rub her back.

"Mom, what's wrong?"

My dad sat across from us and cleared his throat. "Aria, your mother and I have something we need to tell you."

"*You* have something *you* need to tell her," my mother said, spitting the words as if they were poison. "I don't have any part of this."

"Tell me what?" My heart pounded so fast, I thought it might leap from my chest. My father raked his hand through his thinning hair. "Dad, what is it?"

"You…you saw the man talking to me at Mitchell's tonight."

"Yeah?"

A cry escaped from Mom's throat, and she covered her face with her hands. "Dear God, no," she said.

"You guys are really scaring me," I said. "Who was that guy?"

As the child of morticians, I'd seen my share of grief-stricken people. Until I'd realized Macy couldn't see the mysterious stranger at the bar, I had assumed he was a mourning widower who wanted his wife to look just like she had when she was alive and healthy or a devastated father who needed someone to be angry at for his son being gone too soon. It hadn't been the first time one of my dad's grieving clients approached him in public.

Now I wondered who it could be that had my mother so upset. And the question that had been nagging me all night, as Macy and I made our popcorn and picked out a movie and enacted all our slumber party rituals, was front and center in my mind: Why didn't Macy see him?

My dad cleared his throat again.

"That man is dead, Aria. And the fact that you saw him changes absolutely everything."

Chapter Four

"What do you mean he's dead?"

"I mean, he's a ghost, as of late yesterday, and he's quite understandably unhappy and confused about it."

"But...but people can't just...*see* ghosts."

"I can. And now, so can you."

A feral-sounding wail escaped from my mother, and I turned to see her pressing a napkin to her mouth, her chin trembling.

"We'll talk about this more tomorrow, when we have more time and...privacy."

"Tomorrow? But, Dad, you can't just drop this on me and not explain. Why can we see ghosts? What did that man want with you? What is going to change?"

He shook his head and held his hand up in a gesture he'd used to silence my endless questions so often when I was little. "Tomorrow. Macy is waiting for you, and with her level of patience, I expect to see her coming up here any moment to find out what's holding you up."

I looked at my mother, pleading with my eyes for her to change my dad's mind or to tell me something, anything, that would help me make sense of what was happening. Her vacant eyes and downturned mouth told me I shouldn't press it.

I stumbled back to the basement in a daze, got into my sleeping bag, and pushed play on the remote. Before the killer klown could even raise his knife, Macy pushed pause and sat up.

"What's wrong?"

I considered lying and saying nothing, but I'd never been able to keep a secret from my best friend. Instead, I held out my pinkie, and she curled her pinkie around mine in return. We completed the binding contract that signified that what was about to be said must never be shared with anyone else. I paused, put a handful of popcorn in my mouth, and after I swallowed, I told Macy what had transpired.

"Ghosts?" Her enormous brown eyes seemed to take up her whole face. "Are you sure they're not doing some bit that's only funny after you figure out they're messing with you?"

I shook my head. "You should've seen my mom's face. She looked like somebody died." I pressed my lips together when I realized my phrasing was all too appropriate. More than seeing a dead man, I was scared because of my mother's reaction. I'd never seen her the way she was tonight: vacant, devastated, and defeated. Bile churned in my stomach, which was cramping with the pain of trying, in vain, to digest what was happening.

"What happens now?" Macy asked, and I loved her for not questioning the validity of seeing a ghost at Columbus's swankiest restaurant. She and I had been horror movie buffs since we were very small. In middle school, we had even organized a small group of friends to go on "ghost hunting" outings, which had pretty much amounted to us staying up late at someone's house and searching the darkest places with our flashlights and taking notes in spiral notebooks. I'd expected a lot more questions, but she had taken me at my word that I told her everything I knew.

"I don't know," I said. "I guess I'll find out tomorrow."

"Is there anything I can do?"

"You can let me focus on killer klowns and try not to think about this."

She gazed at me for a few moments before nodding and pressing play.

❖

Macy left the next morning, and as soon as she got home, I got a text reminding me of my promise to tell her every detail of the mystery that was unfolding.

After I showered and dressed, I went downstairs and found my mom in the kitchen, sitting exactly where she'd been last night. I would've wondered if she'd been there all night if her hair hadn't been damp from her shower.

"Morning," I said. I walked to the cupboard that held the mugs and got my coffee cup down.

"I haven't made coffee yet," Mom said.

"No problem," I said, trying to act like it wasn't unusual that it was 9:00 a.m., and she hadn't fixed coffee. "I'll make it."

Much like wanting to bury myself in the movie last night, this morning I focused solely on mundane tasks. When I'd showered, I talked myself through every aspect of it and focused on the sound of the water, the smell of my shampoo, the feel of the droplets—turned up as hot as I could stand it—as they bounced off my flesh. I counted every tooth when I brushed, concentrating on the lather, the sharp minty taste, the abrasive scrub of the bristles. Now I was making coffee, and I looked deeply into the dark granules as I scooped them into the filter. I convinced myself that if I focused on what was normal, maybe normal was all that could exist.

When the coffee was ready, I grabbed a mug for my mom and added lots of artificial sweetener and powdered cream. I couldn't stomach my coffee like that, but it was the way she liked it. In my cup, I added a solid pour of butter praline creamer and sat across from her, studying her. She gazed out the sliding glass door, and I turned to see if a hummingbird was at the feeder or a squirrel was on the patio...or even if there was a ghost behind me. There was nothing there, at least not that I could see.

A shiver worked its way up my spine, and I took a big gulp of hot coffee, which did nothing to chase my chill away. I had barely slept all night. The pitch black of the basement had never bothered me before, but every creak and sigh of our old house jerked me awake, gasping panicked breaths and straining in the darkness to try to see if a ghost was lurking above me. Finally, I ended up putting *The Princess Bride* on TV and set it on mute so I wouldn't wake Macy. From time to time, I looked over at my blissfully sleeping friend, and a wash of jealous anxiety poured over me. Ghosts could just walk up to me. Would I ever get a good night's sleep again?

"Good morning." Dad crossed the kitchen to get his own coffee.

"Morning." I glanced at my mom, who raised her cup to her lips to take her first sip, not speaking.

Dad sat beside me and blew into his cup of black liquid. He never added anything. "Dark, like my soul," he always said.

Several moments passed before he gently rested his fingers on my mom's hands. "Joanna," he said softly, "we need to show her." My mother shook her head. "Joanna." My mom yanked her hand away.

"I'm not going," she said. "This is all your…" She stopped and swallowed hard. "This has nothing to do with me. You'll have to show her yourself." With that, she dumped what was left of her coffee into the sink and went upstairs. She didn't slam the bedroom door, but I definitely heard it shut.

"Well," my dad said quietly, "are you ready to go?"

"Where are we going?"

"To the funeral home."

CHAPTER FIVE

My dad turned on the car and reached up to the old-fashioned CD collection strapped to the visor above his head. There was a definite theme to the songs he favored: those performed either by my mom or me. He chose an old performance my mom did at Carnegie Hall in the 1990s. My jaw tightened as I prepared for what I knew he was going to say.

"This. This is the performance where I fell in love with your mother. I knew that day that I was going to marry her." He smiled wistfully. "It only took three years to convince her she was going to marry me."

"Dad, are you and Mom okay?"

He frowned at being removed from his reverie and took a moment to think. "We're not okay right now. But we'll be okay again. You have to understand, this is not what your mother and I planned."

"How can I understand anything when you haven't told me what's going on?"

He rested his fingers on my hand, mirroring the gesture I'd seen him make with Mom earlier. "Soon," he said. "By the end of the day, you'll know everything."

❖

Nick Beckett, my dad's managing funeral director and best friend, met us at the door of the funeral home. The two murmured words I couldn't hear even as much as I strained.

"Aria, we'll be right back," Dad said before hurrying off with him.

I moved out of the doorway and into a small room down the hall. My mother called this room the secondary showroom. When two funerals took place on the same day, this was where we held the one with fewer mourners. When a funeral was going to be very large, we opened the accordion door between this room and the main room and arranged chairs in here. For me, this room carried nostalgic weight, with none of the official titles bearing any importance. It was my playroom when I was small, and both my parents were working, and as I grew older, it was where I would study and read and dream.

I sat on my favorite couch—gargantuan, ancient, green, shiny, and resembling a sea monster—and looked around the room. It could have been any formal living room: plush carpet, comfortable couches, lighting that was both effective and restrained, paintings of cityscapes and lighthouses on the walls. I supposed most formal living rooms didn't have a casket with a body in it, and this one did. On the opposite side of the room, a white-haired woman nestled on soft cushions inside a bronze casket.

I turned to the small table beside the couch, picked up one of the folded bulletins, and began to read about her. Clara Braverman, seventy-three years old, died after a short battle with intestinal cancer. She was a loving mother and grandmother who was preceded in death by her husband, Solomon. She was an avid traveler and bingo player and would be missed by those who loved to listen to her stories and hear her raucous laugh.

I walked over to the casket, looking down at her. Whoever embalmed her and did her hair and makeup had done a really good job. She looked as if she'd gotten dressed in her smartest pale pink suit, taken extra care on her hair and mascara, and then decided to take a nice nap before going out for brunch.

I had a tradition that started when I was a child and was sent to this room to occupy myself while my parents worked. Sometimes the room was empty, but it often held the body of a deceased person at the end of a day after calling hours but before the funeral, the last stop before they went to their final resting place. I found a lot of comfort in saying good-bye and wishing them safe passage on their migration to the afterlife.

I'd forgotten about my tradition. Since I'd gone away to college, I hadn't been coming to the funeral home much. When was the last time? A year, maybe two? I couldn't remember, but I did remember how all my visits to this room started when I wasn't alone in it.

I reached into the casket and rested my hand on Clara Braverman's hand. "Peace on your journey," I said softly.

"Thank you," said a voice beside me.

I screeched and jumped away. When I turned to see who was speaking, it took several moments for my brain to compute. I looked at the woman in the casket and back up to the woman beside me, trying to understand how they could be one and the same.

The smiling lady didn't look like a ghost, or not the way I'd ever seen ghosts look in movies. I couldn't see through her, and she didn't look hazy with blurred edges. She looked…alive. A glance at the woman lying before me confirmed that wasn't possible.

"Mrs. Braverman?" My voice came out papery and thin.

"You can call me Clara, dear."

"Clara." Now what? "You're not wearing your pink suit," I said finally.

Clara looked at the light gray sweat suit and bright white sneakers she wore and adjusted the visor on her head. "We get to choose one outfit to wear while we wait. Since they couldn't give me a definite time frame, I wanted to be comfortable. This is what I wore last time I went hiking at Hocking Hills."

"While you wait?" I asked. "Wait for what?"

I was suddenly angry that she, this ghost, knew more about what was going on here than I did. This place was my family's business, and clearly, there was a lot more to it than I ever knew because they'd kept me completely out of the loop.

"Aria."

My father stood in the doorway with Nick just behind him. They didn't seem angry exactly, but they were very serious. Nick in particular had a peculiar look on his face that I couldn't decipher.

"Oh, Mr. Jasper, Mr. Beckett," Clara cried, rushing to meet them. "Do you have any news on my case?"

My father gave Nick a pointed look, and Nick put his arm out to Clara, ushering her from the room and speaking softly. Once they were gone, I peered into the casket again, confirming the only thing I knew for sure: Clara Braverman was dead.

"Aria," Dad repeated.

"Yes?"

"Come with me." He extended his hand, and I slowly crossed the room and took it. He gave my palm a tight squeeze. "Are you ready?"

I wanted to ask what I was supposed to be ready for or point out that I couldn't prepare myself for something about which I had no details, but instead, I nodded. My stomach, which I'd finally gotten to settle earlier in the morning by focusing on normal tasks, was churning away again. I felt a sudden and intense panic that made me want to run for the door, but I followed my father out of the room.

Chapter Six

I'm not going down there."

I stopped short when I saw where my father was taking me. We stood side by side, staring down into the basement. The basement where they embalmed the bodies. The basement where I'd been told, since the beginning of my life, that I must never go.

Dad flipped a switch, illuminating the oddly cheerful pale blue walls, and put an arm around me.

"We're not going into the embalming room," he said.

"Really?" I could hear the doubt in my voice.

"I promise. None of what you're going to see has anything to do with…that." He took one step down and looked back. I took a deep breath and followed.

At the bottom of the stairs was a small waiting area, and it reminded me of the one at my dentist's office. Chairs stood along the walls of the room. A rack of magazines caught my eye, and I picked one up. It was called *Next Time* and had ads for articles like "10 Tips for a Seamless Transfer" and "Then and Now: Living Your Best Afterlife." I set the magazine back in the rack. A brightly lit lobby that could have been in any office building or doctor's office across the country was definitely not the ghostly basement chamber I had envisioned, and I breathed a jagged sigh of relief.

There was a square window cut into the wall across from

me, and a rosy-cheeked, curly-haired woman slid it open when she noticed us standing there. She gave us a beaming smile when we approached.

"Hi, Nathan," she said brightly. "Who do you have with you today?"

"Sally, this is my daughter, Aria."

Her eyebrows lifted, and her smile widened. "The famous Aria." I took her outstretched hand, and she gave me the most vigorous handshake of my life, pumping my hand up and down like the handle of a three-hole punch.

"I'm famous?" I asked.

"Well, of course." Sally clicked a few keys on her laptop and spun it around so I could see that she was listening to a recording of me. It was playing softly enough that I couldn't hear it until she lifted the computer, but that was my face on the music app. "I've heard so much from your parents about all your talents, and I've downloaded those indie singles of yours. I just can't wait to see where your career takes you."

"Sally," my father said, "Aria is here to begin training."

Sally's eyebrows lifted so far this time, they seemed to be almost in her hairline. "Training?"

"Yes. She experienced her first signs of the quickening yesterday."

"But wasn't yesterday her—"

"Her birthday, yes."

"Oh." Sally's eyebrows dropped. "Oh my."

"Buzz us in, won't you?"

"Of course." Sally reached under her desk and pushed a button, and a glass door a few feet away from her window began to swing inward.

"Follow me," Dad said.

When we walked through, I read the bold navy-blue words on it: Welcome to AfterCorps—Helping millions end their beginning and begin their end.

"First things first," said Dad. "The grand tour. You've seen the waiting room, where the dead wait to be seen by an agent. Over here are small meeting rooms; we use those when we're talking to our clients, both dead and living." He guided me down a short hallway with a door on the left and right and a metal gray door at the end that read Do Not Enter. He opened the door on the left and flipped on the lights so I could see a huge table surrounded by chairs in a room painted a maroon that was way too dark for a basement with no windows.

"Conference room," Dad said. "Where we do our conferencing." I looked up, and he gave me a small smile. He was trying to do the dad joke thing even in the midst of our confusing, intense goings on. Normally, I was a sucker for his jokes, but I couldn't even pull a smile this time. I was too nervous, and the pit of my stomach swirled more violently than before, as if a storm was raging inside.

He turned to the room on the right. When those lights came on, I felt blinded by bright yellow made extreme by the fluorescent bulbs.

"You need to talk to your decorator about these paint jobs." I squeezed my eyes closed and opened them again.

"I am my decorator," Dad said. "And your feedback is duly noted."

When my eyes adjusted, I looked around. It resembled one of my classrooms at school. Well, kind of. There were only four desks, plus one that was presumably for a teacher, and there was an old-school blackboard like I'd only seen in movies and TV. There wasn't a computer anywhere. It was the last kind of space I would've expected to find in the basement of a funeral home. I walked to the teacher's desk and hoisted myself up on it.

"Tell me what's going on." I put my hand on my stomach and willed it to settle, willed my nerves to calm down.

My dad sat gingerly on the edge of one of the student desks. "We've always been open with you about the realities of death," he began and shook his head. "What I mean to say is, we've always been open with you about a part of what happens when someone dies. The part that affects the living. The part of our business you know about, in its essence, is about those still alive. Helping them find ways to honor the deceased so they can say good-bye. Giving them the tools to have a final ceremony and bury their dead so they have closure that allows them to get back to the business of living. It's important work, but it's only one half of what we do." He paused, checking as if to see if I was still with him.

"What's the other part of what you do?"

"We facilitate the transition of the deceased from this world to the next."

I wrinkled my nose. "Can you tell me what that means without sounding like a sales brochure?"

"I'll try. You've heard ghost stories where someone who died can't cross over because they have unfinished business, yes?"

"Yes."

"Well, like most legends, there is something to that. But since the beginning of time, there have been those of us among the living who have the ability to see and communicate with ghosts. Interpreters, if you will. For as long as we've existed, it's been our responsibility to help the dead get their earthly affairs in order as well as work with counterparts on the other side to make the arrangements for their final transfer."

"You make it sound like you work in customs."

He nodded. "It is a bit like that, yes. The whole process is much more bureaucratic than those who romanticize ghost stories would ever imagine. Think of us as Death Agents, a combination of customs, bureau of motor vehicles, police detectives, judiciaries, and social workers."

"And every agent performs all of those jobs?"

"No." He pulled his pack of Juicy Fruit out of his pocket and offered me gum. I shook my head, and he popped a piece in his mouth, his brow wrinkled as he began to chew. "It's sort of like being a musician. You have to learn many different facets of music in your training. The best musicians study classical, jazz, blues, rock, and the list goes on. Very few musicians play or sing in every single genre; they study them and find what speaks to them and what they're good at, and that's where they build their careers.

"Similarly, you'll receive training on many aspects of working with the dead before you choose an area to devote yourself to in your career."

My career? The gravity of what that suggested hit me, and a puff of air bubbled from my chest and escaped my mouth. I felt crushed and flattened as I began to realize the weight of what he was saying. "But, Dad, I already have a career. You know that. I've been studying and practicing my whole life to be a singer." The years of vocal lessons with multiple teachers and constant auditions to gain entry into choirs or musical theater productions, refusing to consume dairy and citrus to avoid their negative impact to my vocal cords and practicing a minimum of four hours a day, these were the things flashing through my mind. What I said was, "What about Angela Osborn? What about Los Angeles?"

"Sweetheart," Dad said softly, "you won't be able to go to Los Angeles."

"Of course I will. I'm twenty-two; you can't keep me here. I don't care what you think I'm able to do with ghosts. I have my life planned out, and that plan doesn't include ghost school."

"Aria, this isn't the case of a father telling his grown daughter what to do. This is an interpreter telling another interpreter that you must stay here and complete your training. There are consequences, not only for you but for me if you don't stay, and they are severe."

"What kind of consequences?"

"I can't tell you. Not yet."

Tears rolled down my cheeks before I even registered them in my eyes. "I don't understand. How did this even happen?"

He sighed. "Normally, future interpreters begin to see the dead at a fairly young age. It can happen as early as sixteen but almost always surfaces by the time someone is nineteen. If someone hasn't shown any signs of a quickening by the time they're twenty, it is almost certain that they didn't inherit the ability to communicate with ghosts. It happens, but it's rare. When you spent so much time here and never saw or spoke to one, your mother and I thought you were a reg—a regular, non-interpreter—like she is."

"So what happened?" I used the sleeve of my jacket to wipe tears away. I was beginning to wish I'd run away from the funeral home when I had the chance.

"In extremely rare cases, an interpreter comes into their quickening after the age of twenty. If it doesn't happen by the time someone turns twenty-two, they never receive any translating abilities."

"But I was twenty-two when I saw the ghost for the first time."

My dad stood and rested his hand on my shoulder.

"Not quite," he said. "You were born at 9:08 p.m. You saw Mr. Pfeiffer around eight o'clock."

"One hour." One hour had made the difference in living the life I had planned since I had cognitive thoughts and living a life devoted to death. The disbelief that had been a constant since last night gave way to horrible belief that my life was ruined. The storm in my stomach overwhelmed me, and I hopped off the desk, rushed past my father, and threw up in the trash can.

Chapter Seven

I texted Macy that night after my parents were in bed, telling her I needed her to come over. I sat in the living room, watching for her car. When she arrived, we shuffled down to the basement.

When we were little, we used to pretend the basement was our apartment. The finished section had a family room, small guest bedroom, and bathroom, and it was the site of our most epic slumber parties. Most of them, my parents knew about, but some they didn't. We started using the space after our first sleepover, when our incessant giggling kept my mom awake until nearly three in the morning. When my parents were asleep in their second-floor bedroom, and Macy and I were in the basement, they couldn't hear us at all. It had been a blessing to them when we were little and convenient for us when we were older.

I noticed the bulge in the long front pocket of her hoodie. "What's that?"

"Emergency sustenance." She grinned and pulled out two forty-ounce cans of beer. Ignoring the way my stomach still twisted, I took one and opened it, downing several gulps. "Jesus, take it easy," Macy said.

"You won't be saying that once you hear about my day." I drained about half my forty, burped, and it echoed against the walls. Funny how even finished basements were more echoey than rooms in the rest of the house.

"Okay, so tell me." Macy sipped her own beer.

Earlier, I'd had slight pause about whether to tell her about AfterCorps and the news my dad dropped. He didn't explicitly say not to talk to her about it, but he did discuss the secrecy surrounding the organization. In the end, I didn't really care what he thought about my sharing it with Macy, and I needed someone sane and outside of this situation to talk to. I started at the beginning with my mom's non-coffee making, damp-haired stares, and brought her the welcome packet my dad gave me after dropping the bomb that I would be trading in my previously scheduled life for this new, subpar existence.

Macy opened the folder and took out the top sheet of paper, reading it out loud. "Welcome to your exciting new career at AfterCorps!" She pronounced the second part of the word like "corpse," and when I told her it was pronounced "core," she shrugged and said, "My way makes more sense." I couldn't disagree.

"You will learn how to liaise between the dead and living and accomplish the goals most important to your clients, as well as complete the correct paperwork and documentation necessary to assist in making their final transfer. You'll get hands-on experience navigating the emotional needs of the newly deceased and gain solid defense techniques against unsavory customers." Macy arched an eyebrow. "God. This reads like a college catalogue."

"Yeah. I'll be attending the Worst Nightmare University."

Macy set the paper down. "So no LA."

I shook my head. "Instead of spending my summer in Los Angeles getting my music career started, I'll be in the basement at the funeral home learning Ghost Paperwork in Triplicate 101." I'd felt numb since my dad unloaded the news, after the initial crying spree and vomiting episode. I'd only heard about half of what he said after that, lost in visions of singing onstage in front of thousands of fans, the story I'd told myself every night before I fell asleep now becoming no more than a fairy tale.

"What happens if you say no at the end of your training?" Macy asked.

"What do you mean?"

Macy rolled her eyes. "Whenever someone realizes they have special gifts in a story, there comes a moment when they have to decide whether to be the superhero or whether they're going to go back to being whoever they were before they realized they were special. They always choose superhero on TV because it makes for better entertainment, but what if you decided to just be Aria Jasper, really awesome singer?"

I took a long pull on my beer. "I have no idea." I hadn't thought of that. My father had been so absolute in his revelations that it hadn't occurred to me to think about taking a couple years to do my training, pacify my dad, and go back to the plan I had for my life. I felt a spark of hope, albeit a small one, that all wasn't lost.

"You should probably find out."

CHAPTER EIGHT

A week after I graduated from NYU, when I should have been packing my suitcase in preparation for my move across the country, I got in my Honda Civic and drove to Jasper Funeral Home.

"I'll be there later," my dad had said when I was leaving. He'd handed me a brown lunch bag. I'd looked inside and saw a bologna sandwich, a mandarin orange, and a pickle. "I'm doing the best I can, kid," he'd said when I rolled my eyes.

"I can make my own lunch."

I'd talked to my parents about getting a job so I could move into my own place. If I wasn't going to start my dream career, I at least wanted to have a space of my own.

"Why don't we talk about it after you have a few months of training under your belt?" Dad had said. "It's going to be fairly intense, and you may not have time to get a job that would give you enough hours to make rent."

I was starting to get the uneasy feeling that my dad was trying to stunt me somehow. Between not wanting me to move out to making me lunches in brown paper bags, it seemed as if he wanted me to be a kid again. I had no idea why or what it meant and got nothing but skilled sidestepping whenever I confronted him about it.

I'd barely seen my mom since graduation. When I did see her, she was always at the kitchen table, her hair usually damp, as if she needed to wash something away before venturing out of her room. My dad and I took turns making her toast or slicing grapefruits and sliding them in front of her to nibble on. She spoke in hushed monotones, tears trickling from her eyes like a cracked glass filled with water, leaking so slightly that you almost didn't notice until you picked it up and found your palm damp.

When I'd asked my dad what was happening to her, he'd talked about how badly my mom wanted me to follow in her footsteps and be a singer and how disappointed she was that those dreams had been replaced. I didn't buy it. Sure, my mom had been a singer in her younger days, and she was proud of me, but I had never felt like she needed me to continue on the trail she blazed. Besides, she gave up singing professionally when she married my dad and became a mortician. It made no sense that she'd be devastated at the prospect of a daughter who was a death worker. I didn't push the issue, not yet.

I was exhausted from being scared and worried all the time, and my training hadn't even started yet. My dad was almost certainly lying to me, my mom was severely depressed with no sign of any improvement, and my lifelong goals had been indefinitely shelved. As if all that wasn't bad enough, I was now peering around every corner, startled at every noise, convinced a ghost was going to attack. My father assured me it wasn't going to happen, but he was being so mysterious about everything, I didn't feel I could trust him. That hurt too, probably more than anything else. I'd never felt like I couldn't trust my parents to have my back or support me, and I'd lost that.

I went inside the funeral home and down to the basement. Sally stood when she saw me arriving, but before I could get to her, I heard a voice say, "Hello again, dear." I turned and saw Clara sitting in one of the chairs, a magazine in her hands.

"Hello, Ms. Braverman," I said.

"Clara."

"Clara." I calculated how long it had been since I met her. Almost three weeks. "I'm surprised to see you still here."

"Oh, you know," she said, waving her hand. "A delay with my paperwork is all. In fact, I'm hoping to get everything resolved sometime today, and then I'll be on my way."

The sound of glass on glass distracted me, and Sally slid the window to the side and waved me toward her.

"I guess I need to be going," I said. "Nice to see you again, Clara."

"Lovely to see you, dear."

Sally stood when I got to her desk. "You're late," she said, not unkindly.

"It's nine o'clock. I'm on time."

"You need to be at your desk promptly at nine. Your classmate has been here for nearly half an hour. *She* was on time."

"My classmate?" This was the first I was hearing about anyone else training with me. Since most people had their quickening so much younger, I'd get private lessons. If I started with other newly empowered interpreters, I'd be surrounded by much smaller kids.

"Oh God, it's not some fifteen-year-old, is it?" I asked. "Please tell me I'm not going to be doing this terrible training and also babysitting at the same time."

Sally stiffened. "She's not fifteen. And this isn't terrible. There is no more honorable work than what you'll be learning to do, young lady."

"Sorry," I said, trying to mean it.

Sally frowned and reached down beneath her desk to buzz me in. "Go on back."

"Thank you."

My classmate was *definitely* not fifteen. She was sitting in the desk nearest the door when I walked in and had short shaggy hair. It was light brown, as opposed to my raven-colored waves. She wore baggy jeans, bright blue Converse, and a T-shirt with a band I'd never heard of on the front. She turned and gave me a crooked smile. She was gorgeous.

"Hey," she said. "I'm Sloane."

"Aria. Hi."

"So," she said after I'd been standing in the doorway staring for a few seconds, "you wanna come in?" She waved at the empty desks. "There are plenty of choices."

"Oh yeah." I felt a blush rise to my cheeks. "Thanks." I chose the desk to her left and sat.

"Aria Jasper, right?"

"Right." The heat on my cheeks spread to my neck when I heard my name on her lips. "How did you know?"

"You're the reason I get to finally start my training." More crooked smiling from her and blushing from me. Then her words registered, and I frowned.

"What do you mean?" I asked.

Sloane pulled a battered workbook out of a backpack at her feet. "This has been the extent of my training for the last year," she said. I took the workbook and looked through it, noting that the pages had furious notes scribbled into every available space. "By the time I had my quickening, I was too old to start traditional interpreter classes. My mom gave me this book, and between that and the little hands-on work she's let me try, I thought I'd be stuck as a clerk forever. Now I have a chance to be a special." I must have looked as lost as I felt because her eyes widened. "You don't understand a word of this, do you?"

"Maybe a handful of the words. That's about it."

"You're telling me the daughter of the top leader in the organization doesn't know the first thing about AfterCorps?"

I was embarrassed and wanted to direct her attention away from me. "How long have you known about it?"

"When have I *not* known about it?" she said and shrugged. "I've been planning to be an interpreter since I could walk. I was so scared when I turned eighteen, and my quickening hadn't happened yet. And when I turned twenty and still nothing, I almost gave up."

"So when did it happen?"

"About three months before I turned twenty-two."

I thought about seeing the frantic stranger talking to my dad at the bar at Mitchell's and my dad trying to communicate while also attempting to appear as if he wasn't talking to himself. "Quickening" sounded like a dramatic event, and I'd been wondering if it was as mundane an experience for others as it had been for me.

"What was it like? Your quickening?" I asked.

She opened her mouth to answer when a voice boomed in the doorway beside us. "Sorry I'm late." It was Nick.

Normally, he wore business suits in gray or black for the funeral home and sweats or basketball shorts if he and my dad were hanging out. Today, he had on fitted jeans and an untucked checkered button-down shirt beneath a sweater vest. It was a drastically different look for him, and it was weird.

"Hey Nick," I said.

He walked to the front of the room and set his messenger bag on the desk. "Hey, girl," he said, his standard greeting for me. To Sloane, he said, "Sorry, we haven't met. I'm Nick Beckett, and you are?"

"Sloane Dennison." She stood and shook his hand. She seemed starstruck and held on a little too long; her eyes and mouth were wide. I wondered what kind of rock star Nick was to have my new crush looking at him like that.

"Great," he said. "Sloane, Aria, I'll be administering your lessons for the foreseeable future. Welcome to Ghost School." He went to the blackboard and wrote the word "Quickening" in lumpy uneven letters. "Who can tell me what a quickening is?"

"The thing that ruined my life," I said.

He tipped his head to the side. "It changed your life, to be sure. Time will tell if your life will be ruined, and if it is, it'll be done by your attitude and not your gifts."

Ouch.

"Sloane," Nick said, pointing with the piece of chalk. "What's a quickening?"

"It's the moment at which someone first comes into their

interpreter powers," she answered. "It happens through the first communication with a prior, either visually or audibly, and in some cases, both, although it's rare to experience both in a quickening."

"Good."

"Wait, what's a prior?" I asked.

"It's an AfterCorps-specific term for a ghost. We are living, so we're currents. They are priors."

"Okay," I said. "And...you said it's rare to be able to both see and hear a ghost during your quickening?"

"It occurs in slightly less than ten percent of quickenings," he said. "Did you guys experience visual or audible?"

"Both," Sloane and I said in unison.

"Maybe it's not so rare," she said with a laugh.

"Trust me, it's rare." Nick eyed us thoughtfully. "It's about as common as left handedness."

"I'm left-handed," I said.

"Oh my God, me too!" Indeed, she was holding her pen in her left hand just like I was.

"We're cosmically linked," I said, blushing before the words were completely out of my mouth.

"Obviously," she said with a grin, and I felt my toes twinkling with happiness inside my shoes.

I heard the staccato sound of chalk on blackboard and looked up to see Nick write the words "In-class assignment."

"Today is the first day of your training, and like any first day, introductions are key. I want the two of you to write about your quickenings using every detail you can remember. Then tell a little bit about yourselves. You can finish with telling some things you know about AfterCorps already and what you hope to learn while I'm working with you. This will help guide my lessons. There are some things I'll be teaching you regardless, per AfterCorps guidelines, but since there are only two of you, and you're older, things will be a little different than if you'd started in a class of half a dozen sixteen-year-olds.

"For one thing, since you are older, we'll need to do an accelerated version of your studies. You'll start getting hands-on experience a lot sooner. Finally, I'll have the liberty to custom design a part of your coursework in accordance with your strengths and interests."

He moved behind his desk, pulled a notebook out of his messenger bag, and sat. "I'll be writing too. I'll make copies at the end for all of us to take home, and each of us will have two other assignments to read this evening as homework."

I glanced at Sloane, who was already scribbling, a small smile on her face. I shook my head at how happy she was to be starting ghost lessons and opened my notebook to begin my own work.

CHAPTER NINE

I got home that afternoon, a little giddy from sitting next to Sloane all day. She was definitely the bright spot in all of this. Sloane and orange juice.

I loved orange juice with a passion, but I rarely got to drink it. Citrus was rough on the vocal cords, especially near a performance, and since I always had a performance just around the corner, I could've counted on one hand the number of times I'd gotten to drink orange juice before my quickening.

Since I'd come into my abilities, I started keeping a gallon of OJ in the fridge at all times. I went to the kitchen, poured a giant glass, and sat at the table. There was a growing stack of mail since Mom had always been the one to handle bills and correspondence. I took a gulp of juice and looked through the envelopes. When I came across one addressed to me from MoodWave Media, I set my glass down with a *thunk*, and a bit of the thick liquid sloshed onto my hand. I stared at the envelope for a while. It could have been seconds or hours. Finally, I opened it and began to read.

Dear Aria Jasper:
We are sorry to hear you have decided against pursuing your music career. Any agreements regarding

*your future at MoodWave Media, whether verbal or in
writing, have now been terminated.*
    Best of luck in all your future endeavors.
    Sincerely,
    Angela Osborn

I trembled as I read the letter five times, then ten. My father
had been vague when I talked to him about training for a few
years and leaving the option open to go back into music once I
fulfilled my duties to AfterCorps. It hadn't occurred to me that
there might not be a music career to go back to when I was done.

I had laid my AfterCorps homework on the table too and
noticed a large drop of orange juice on the paper. When I wiped
it away, it made a long streak across Nick's words about his
quickening. I stared at that streak while I finished my juice, then
got up and put my glass in the sink and threw the Moodwave letter
in the trash. That small act shattered me. I stared into the trash
can and cried, my whole body shaking with the impact of this
latest crushing blow. How could this be happening? I'd always
known what I wanted in my life, and I'd worked and sacrificed so
much for it. Not a single day went by that I didn't put everything
I had into pursuing music. How could it all be gone?

I walked upstairs, past my parents' closed bedroom door—
my mother was no doubt in bed—and went into my bedroom.
Sitting on the edge of my bed, I could see the door to my parents'
bedroom, and glared at it. My life was falling apart, and instead
of offering support or comfort, my mom was hiding. I wanted to
hide too, but I couldn't, and I was so angry and lonely. The only
people who could really help me with what I was going through
were both closing themselves off from me in their own ways, and
I didn't know why.

I closed my door and walked to the music stand in the corner.
Sheet music for the last piece I'd been practicing, "I'm Not That
Girl" from *Wicked*, sat open, a light film of dust on the pages. I

hadn't practiced since I found out that nothing I'd planned for my life was going to happen anymore.

I sat at my small electric keyboard and turned it on. I stumbled through the piano intro for the song—I'd always been a better singer than pianist, and I'd gotten rusty these last few weeks—and began to sing. I got nearly to the end before I broke again into deep, lung-crushing tears. Never had I felt so hopeless, so far removed from my own life.

Not bothering to turn off my keyboard, I crawled onto my bed and wrapped a corner of my cheerful teal and orange plaid comforter over me. The name was a misnomer, as I didn't feel even a little comforted. By the time the tears had stopped rolling down my cheeks, I had fallen asleep.

❖

I woke in the middle of the night, hungry and shivering. I changed into pajamas and my black terry cloth robe and went downstairs to the kitchen. A light was on, and to my surprise, I found my mom sitting at the table. She was bent over my homework, reading.

"Mom?" She jumped. "Sorry, I didn't mean to scare you."

"It's all right." She looked back at the papers and stood, coming around the table to give me a hug. "Do you want something to eat?"

"Sure." I was surprised. She hadn't cooked a meal since my birthday disaster, but I was too hungry to rock the boat by asking why she suddenly wanted to make food for me.

She went to the fridge and rummaged around. "Hmm," she said, her voice muffled by the contents, "there's not much to choose from." She pulled her head out and held some eggs, cheese, onions, and mushrooms. "An omelet okay?"

"Sounds great." The bottom had officially fallen out of my stomach.

I watched her pull out a skillet and busy herself making omelets. "I'll go to the store tomorrow and get us restocked," she said. "Any requests?"

"I'm almost out of orange juice."

She paused, her spatula in midair. Then she flipped the eggs and gave a quick nod. "I'll get you some more."

Soon, she set a plate with an enormous omelet in front of me and sat across from me, using her fork to cut a bite.

"Thanks, Mom." I took a bite, and a strand of gooey cheese hung out of my mouth and rested on my chin. I tucked it between my lips and swallowed. "This is so good."

"I'm glad you like it." She smiled around her food and set her fork down. "Aria, I'm sorry. I know that I've…that I took this news very hard, and I haven't been here for you."

"It's okay."

She shook her head forcefully. "It's not okay. I'm your mother. I've never let you go through anything alone, and I shouldn't have let you go through this without me."

I cut a few pieces of egg and pushed them around on my plate while I thought about what to say. "Why are you so upset about this?"

She faltered, and her gaze slipped from my eyes to her plate.

"This was your future, Aria. Your destiny. I thought, after you turned eighteen, that we were safe, and you could pursue music and have a normal life. And when we made it to your twenty-second birthday, I woke up feeling like every weight I'd carried that you'd have to be a…an interpreter, was gone. You were free. I'd been carrying that email from Angela Osborn around in my pocket until your birthday, just to be on the safe side."

"So it's just about my singing?"

"It's about your *life*. I thought your life was going to be your own." She gave a shaky sigh. "But you belong to AfterCorps now."

"Belong to them?" That sounded bad. I knew so little about

what was happening to me, and I wondered if I was being kept in the dark to keep me from realizing the enormity of what, exactly, I was losing in all of this. I had lost my dreams of being a musician, but I hadn't stopped to consider that maybe that was the least of it.

"Aria."

I turned and saw my dad in the doorway. I hadn't heard him come downstairs. His pajamas were rumpled, and his hair messy, but his eyes were clear. "I think it's time you went to bed. It's late, and you have class in the morning."

I thought about telling him I was twenty-two and could decide for myself when I went to bed, but something in his eyes stopped me.

I picked up my plate, scarfing down a few more bites as I walked to the sink. On the way out of the kitchen, I grabbed my homework and took a last look at my parents, who seemed to have entered into a staring contest, before going upstairs to my room.

I left my door open and lingered for a moment to see if I could hear what my parents were saying, but it was no use. I could hear the faint sound of their hushed voices every so often but couldn't make out any words. Eventually, I gave up and sat at my desk with the homework sheet in front of me.

Staring without really seeing it, I thought about my parents. Throughout my life, I could remember a handful of arguments, none of which had ever seemed that intense, nor had they ever lasted very long. Certainly there had never been a long stretch of time in which there was palpable tension, as there was now. Of all the things that made me worried about what I was getting into with AfterCorps, their strained relationship combined with my mom's absence the last few weeks were the things that made me most frightened, even more than the possibility that ghosts might be lurking anywhere, at any time.

I scrubbed my eyes and tried to shake off the feeling that

things were going from bad to worse in my house. My homework didn't seem like it would take long, but I needed to finish it and get some sleep.

I set Nick's paper aside and pulled out Sloane's sheet. She had covered the entire front and half the back in tiny print, leaving me to wonder how my own essay, which barely took up three-fourths of a page with my handwriting, would compare when Nick had them side by side.

To be fair, Sloane had grown up learning about AfterCorps and her potential paranormal powers. She'd had years to ask questions and form opinions about what to expect when she made it to her training. She'd obviously been dreaming her whole life about being a special, whatever that was. Two out of the three questions we'd been asked for this assignment had referred to what we already knew and what we wanted to study, and it wasn't my fault that my answers to those were nothing and nothing.

I read her paper and discovered a few interesting things. She'd been working at her mom's flower shop when she had her quickening. They were delivering flowers to a funeral home when a young guy asked Sloane if she had a lighter, and her mom pulled her aside and told her the guy was a ghost. Sloane's mom told the ghost they didn't smoke and directed him into the funeral home for assistance. They'd finished their delivery and then Sloane's mom took her out for a beer to celebrate.

I also learned that Sloane felt she fell low on the AfterCorps hierarchy, but she was determined to work hard and prove she was an elite interpreter. Her ultimate goal was to join the ranks of a sector called CDU, of which Nick was a top officer. That explained the stars in her eyes when she met him.

Nick had encouraged us to make notes on each other's papers, so I grabbed my pen, skimmed her paper again, and jotted these thoughts down:

1. *What is the CDU?*
2. *What are the levels of the AfterCorps hierarchy?*

3. *How do we even know when a quickening happens?*

Sloane and I knew because we were with our interpreter parents, and they noticed us noticing ghosts. Maybe we'd been seeing ghosts before and didn't even know they were dead.

4. *Why would a ghost need a lighter?*

I set Sloane's paper aside and picked up Nick's. His handwriting was jagged but orderly, like a set of knives arranged across the page. His quickening story was a little vague, saying that he and his mom were out shopping at City Center, the mall that used to be in downtown Columbus before it went out of business. A woman came over to Nick when he was trying on school clothes and asked if she could help him find anything, and his mom took the woman to a corner of the fitting room and began whispering to her. Later, his mom explained that the woman was an LG, and that she had directed her back to her SW.

He also referenced being a leader of the CDU and made a point of saying he was the first in his family to have a high ranking AfterCorps job, as his relatives had all been clerks.

I got out my pen for more notes.

5. *Is LG a lost ghost? If so, how exactly does a ghost get lost?*
6. *What is an SW?*
7. *How did Nick go about breaking through barriers to reach such an elevated status?*

I yawned and pulled out my phone to check the time. I was shocked to find it was almost 2:00 a.m. and realized my earlier nap must have been a lot longer than I thought.

Macy had texted me around six to ask how my first day went, then again at nine to ask if I was okay. My thumbs flicked as I typed a quick response.

Day one was okay. It wasn't summer in Los Angeles, but what can you do? I met a total cutie pie, I'll give you details tomorrow, xo.

I went to bed thinking about Sloane's crooked smile and tried to shut out thoughts of how strained my parents were in the kitchen.

CHAPTER TEN

Sally waved and smiled when she reached down to buzz me in the next morning. I went through the glass doors and turned right, heading toward my classroom.

"Aria?" Sally poked her head out of her cubby.

"Yeah?"

She looked a little sheepish. "I wondered, could you sign this for me?"

"Sure, is it some paperwork for training?"

"Uh, no." She pulled out a program from when I performed as the featured soloist with the Columbus Symphony last year. "I was so far up in the balcony that by the time I got through the line to where you'd been greeting people and signing programs, you were already gone."

I took the pen and signed the program. My heart twisted as I looked at my name on the thick, luxuriously buttery paper, above the songs I performed. I should have appreciated those moments onstage more. I performed so often that it always seemed as if there would be an infinite number of instances where I stood in center stage, a spotlight on me and a crowd before me. If I'd known how limited those times were, I would have spent more seconds smiling into the audience before I started to sing, held the last note of every song a little longer, and bowed more deeply. The disbelief I'd felt since finding out about AfterCorps was beginning to subside, and what replaced it was anger at the injustice that my life no longer belonged to me.

"I don't think that signature's going to be worth anything now," I told Sally, and my voice wobbled.

She smiled. "It's worth something to me."

I tried to return her smile, gave her a quick nod, and went toward my classroom.

"Good morning, sunshine," Sloane said when I entered the room.

"Good morning…moonbeam," I replied, and she laughed.

She was wearing a different graphic T-shirt, presumably with another band, although they weren't familiar to me at all. Their name seemed apropos for our current situation.

"Jonesing for Death, huh?"

"Yeah. You know them?"

"Nope."

"Oh, you have to listen!" She pulled her phone out of her pocket and I saw that they had earbuds plugged into them. As she started scrolling through her phone, she handed them to me. "Put these in your ears."

"Why can't you just play it out loud?"

"It's not the same experience."

I shrugged and put the earbuds in. Soon, a mellow guitar riff flowed into my ears, and a man with a gruff and sultry voice started singing about an alien who fell in love with a girl from Earth.

I could bring you all the stars,
Jupiter, Venus, or Mars,
I need you always with me,
We can rule the galaxy.

I started laughing. "You've got to be kidding with this!"

"Why would I be kidding?" Sloane didn't laugh, but she was grinning.

"Those are some sappy lyrics, my friend."

"Oh. I get it." She took the phone and earbuds back from me, her eyes never leaving my face.

"Get what?"

"You've never been in love."

My mouth closed with a pop. I didn't know how to respond to her; she definitely wasn't wrong. Fortunately, Nick chose that moment to enter the classroom.

He clapped a single time. "Okay, guys. How did you do with your assignments? Let me see them."

We handed them over and waited while he took a moment to read. I glanced at Sloane, who was doodling in her notebook. A lock of hair fell across her eye, and she blew it off her face and back into the shaggy mop on top of her head. I wondered if she had any idea how cute she was, then remembered her slightly cocky grin from a few moments ago. Oh yeah, she knew.

"Aria," Nick said, "you forgot part of your assignment."

"What do you mean?"

He turned my paper to show it to me. "You only answered my first question. I still need at least an overview of what you know about AfterCorps and what areas in the organization you're interested in exploring."

"But, Nick, I don't know anything. My father didn't tell you?"

"What do you mean, you don't know anything?"

"I mean, I didn't know AfterCorps was even a thing until after I saw my first ghost on my birthday. I never knew my dad was anything other than a normal funeral director or that ghosts were a real thing until then."

Nick's mouth dropped open. "You're joking."

"I'm really not."

His mouth popped closed, his eyes narrowed, and he dropped his head into his hands, muttering, "Really, Nathan?" Finally, he lifted his head. "All this time, your father told me not to talk about AfterCorps because he didn't want to upset you, and in reality, you don't know the first thing about who you are or where you come from."

"Upset me?" I had never been more confused.

His lips flattened into a thin line. "I don't feel comfortable going forward with training until I speak to your father about this." He reached into his messenger bag and pulled out two thin, ancient-looking textbooks. "Here. You guys can start looking at these. I was going to assign the first two chapters for you to read tonight; go ahead and do that. AfterCorps training is suspended until further notice."

"Suspended?" Sloane asked. "How long do you think it's going to be?"

"Until I can get all of this cleared up." He walked out, leaving Sloane and me to gape at each other.

"Wow," I said, mostly just to break the silence.

I thought for a moment that Sloane wasn't going to respond, she paused for so long, staring. "You really didn't know anything about AfterCorps until now? Or even anything about priors?"

"No, I didn't." She continued to stare until I began to feel uncomfortable. "I guess I don't understand what the big deal is."

"The big deal is, most people who have interpreter parents grow up hearing about it from when they learn how to listen. I've been taught about the responsibilities, powers, and traditions that come with being an interpreter since I was potty-trained."

I thought about that. "But you said that not everyone with interpreter parents has a quickening, right? So what if you'd learned all that, and you turned out to be a reg?"

"Then I still would've known about my family's history, my heritage. I would have known the truth about who my mom is and what she does, not just the superficial version of her." I think she saw that part hurt me a little, the thought that I didn't really know my dad, so she switched gears. "Besides, being an interpreter comes with some pretty nonstandard business hours. How did your dad explain that?"

"My dad is a funeral director. Nonstandard hours come with

the territory." Although, now that she'd brought it up, I wondered how often my dad was gone from home on mortuary business and how often it had been AfterCorps business.

"Yeah, that makes sense," Sloane said.

I looked at the textbook. It had a faded pale blue cover with the words *Cognitive Interpretation: Book One*.

"I guess *Talking to Ghosts for Dummies* was already taken," I said, but before Sloane had the chance to respond, I saw the words at the bottom of the cover and gasped. "Written by Myron Jasper!"

"Your great-great-grandfather literally wrote the book on modern interpretation at AfterCorps," Sloane said.

Every time I thought I knew the extent to which my parents had hidden reality from me, I got hit with a new piece of information that proved me wrong. What I'd learned in the last few minutes made my chest feel hollow. Not only had my parents kept me in the dark, but apparently, that was completely the opposite of what most interpreters did. To top that off, one of my relatives had written the handbook on working with ghosts. The worst part about these revelations was that they just created more questions in my mind, like exactly how powerful was my family in AfterCorps, and why hadn't I been brought up being educated like other interpreters' kids?

Since the night of my birthday, I'd felt as if a hole had been burned into my chest. With every new blow, that hole was getting bigger and bigger, something that would eventually turn me inside out and swallow me up if things kept going the way they had been. I put my hand to my heart to reassure myself with its steady, rhythmic beating, and willed myself to stop wondering how much worse this mess would get before it got better.

Chapter Eleven

Since ghost classes were canceled, Sloane and I packed our stuff, got out of the basement, and stepped out into a bright sunny day.

"What are you gonna do now?" she asked.

I shrugged. "I don't know. I guess I'll go home."

She fiddled with her keys. "Do you want to maybe study together or something?"

I'd thought her eyes were pale blue, but now that we were out of the fluorescent-lit basement, they were actually sort of gray, like the sky in the middle of winter, reflecting the snow. "Study?"

"Look, I've been waiting my whole life to start my training. We've barely begun, and now we're stopped. I'm ready to get going. We have our textbooks, right? So maybe we can work together. Besides, I might be able to help you."

"Help me how?"

"Your family hasn't exactly shared a lot with you. They've blanked you out on AfterCorps, and I can help you fill in the blanks. That way, maybe by the time training starts up again, you'll be a little more prepared and a little less shell-shocked."

"It's that obvious, huh?" She smiled. "Sure, okay. Let's study."

"Rock on," she said. "Your house or mine?"

"Hmm. How are the snacks at your house?"

"My house is ruled by Queen Betty Crocker and Princess Little Debbie," she said with a perfectly straight face.

"You know, when she becomes queen, you'll have to start calling her Debra," I said.

"See, I have a lot to learn from you too," Sloane said, the right side of her lips bending upward. "My house, then?"

"I'll follow you there."

❖

Her house was a cute pale yellow bungalow just north of the Ohio State University campus on a sleepy street. She opened the front door and walked in, holding it open for me. It was cozy on the inside, with lots of cushy furniture in the living room.

"Snacks first, then study?" she asked.

"Definitely."

I followed her to a sunny kitchen where she opened a cupboard door, and I burst out laughing at all the Little Debbie cakes.

"But where's Queen Crocker?" I asked.

"If we feel like baking later, you'll get to see her." She tossed me a packaged cupcake. "You want something to drink? Water or pop?"

"Water is cool," I said. She grabbed two bottled waters and sat at the table. I sat across from her and opened my cupcake.

"Are your parents at work?" I asked.

"My mom is. My folks are divorced." She took a sip of water. "He travels a lot for work, so I only see him a few times a month."

"You're close to both of them?"

She nodded slowly. "In different ways, yeah. My mom is a total hippie, always talking about openness and communication, always encouraging me to be my highest self. My dad is all about business and success. He's really into teaching me about being responsible and working hard. They're good people, really different people. They split when I was very young. I can't remember them together, and I can't really picture them together, either."

"I couldn't ever picture my parents apart," I said and frowned. That had always been true, but after the last few weeks, I felt unsure about it for the first time. Uneasiness had become the constant undercurrent in the sea of feelings that had flooded me in the last month, and it flashed up at this new realization.

"So," she said, "wanna get started?" She picked up her backpack and pulled out the textbook, her notebook, and to my surprise, the assignments we turned in to Nick. I hadn't even seen her take them.

"Sure."

"First, why don't I take a look at the questions you had so we can spend this afternoon starting to get you up to speed? Then tonight, we can each read the first two chapters. If school isn't back in session tomorrow, we can at least meet up and talk about them." She leaned over the slightly wrinkled pages and began to read. I looked around the kitchen and saw a picture on the fridge. I walked over and took it out from under the magnet. It was Sloane at maybe six or seven, and there was a blond boy a few years older with her.

"Who's this?" I asked when she'd finished.

"That's my brother, Derek."

"Where's he now?"

"He goes to Tulane for grad school; he's staying in New Orleans this summer for an internship."

I arched my eyebrow. "He's not…"

"An interpreter? Nope. He's not sad about it, either. He never wanted the gift, and he didn't get it. We both got what we wanted."

"Must be nice."

Her eyes darkened for a moment, but she didn't respond, instead picking up a page. "I'm going to answer the questions you asked on my paper in reverse order. Why would a ghost need a lighter? He wouldn't, but sometimes, they get confused. Some ghosts understand that they are dead, and some have a harder time with it. It seems weird, but most of the time, priors are really clearheaded when they first die. The longer they have to stay in this world before the transfer, the more difficult it gets for them. They lose grip on reality, lose the ability to make sense of where they are, why they're here, and what is happening around them. That's part of why interpreters are so important. The quicker we can get them transferred, the more likely it is that they'll relocate without having issues."

The thought of ghosts getting confused and losing their grip on reality sounded absolutely terrifying. I rubbed my arms to try to rid them of the goose bumps that had prickled to the surface.

"Okay," I said. "Is it okay if I take some notes?"

"Sure."

I got my notebook out and scribbled away. "Got it. What next?"

"In question three, you ask how we know when a quickening happens, and your theory was headed in the right direction. The quickening occurs only when you are with the person from whom you inherited interpreting abilities."

I looked up. "Really?"

"Yep. It's nature's way of helping us, if you think about it. Let's say someone's interpreter parent dies. The kid turns sixteen, and they start seeing ghosts who need help, and they don't know what to do, and they're just plain scared shitless, like the kid in *The Sixth Sense*. It would be pretty messed up, right?"

"It would be horrible."

"Exactly. So if the ability to communicate with priors dies with the parent, the kid isn't left to fend for themselves. Our own biology keeps us safe from having to figure it out on our own."

I could feel my blush, and for the first time since I'd met her, it wasn't because she was adorable. Biology hadn't kept me from being blindsided by all of this or from trying to have to muddle my way through it with very little help from my parents. I was so damn mad at them.

On top of being a musician, I'd also been a straight A student my entire life. Macy used to say it was like I was programmed to overachieve because I couldn't not be hyper-focused and hyper-prepared for everything. I couldn't believe my mom and dad had let me walk into something so major without any idea how to handle it.

"Sorry," she said. "I should have said that a different way."

"Don't be sorry. You're doing me a favor. At this point, I've learned more from you than I have from anyone."

She reached across the table and squeezed my hand, and then I was blushing for the same old reason again.

"Now," she said, picking the paper up. "In question two, you asked about the levels in the AfterCorps hierarchy. This is a little more complicated because there are two facets to it. There's the surface job situation, of course."

"The what?"

She shook her head. "You really are clueless."

I scowled. "That's not my fault, remember?"

"You're right," she said, and I forgave her when I saw that crooked smile. "I'm sorry. Surface jobs are the ones everyone connected to AfterCorps has to have. They are the careers that allow us to have something to say when a reg asks what we do, and they are also the jobs that give us access to priors."

I thought about that. My parents were morticians. Sloane's mom was a florist. Nick's mother had run the printing shop that supplied the funeral home with the programs, bulletins, and signature books. "Who else?"

"Well, let's see. Hair and makeup artists, casket salespeople, caterers, clergy, musicians...I'm guessing that'll be your surface profession."

"What?"

"Well, you sing, right? Almost every funeral has music, lots of it live. I'd imagine it would be easy for you to get hired to perform at the services."

I rested my head in my hands. Oh no. When I decided I wanted to move away from my classical, operatic voice training and focus more on pop music, my mom was really understanding. Opera was her love, but she didn't mind that I had a different one. "Just be careful," she'd warned, looking as if she was trying to keep the laughter out of her voice before she delivered the punchline. "You don't want to end up a wedding singer."

It had only been funny because it wasn't going to happen. She knew I'd die before that. But here I was, about to become a death singer, something far, far worse. I felt weak and light-headed. My heart pounded, and I had to squeeze my eyes shut to fight tears away. That hole in my chest seemed to expand farther, and I felt dangerously close to losing myself to something I couldn't see but was there all the same.

Finally, I lifted my face to see Sloane watching with concern.

"Go on," I said.

"You sure?"

"Yeah. Those are the surface jobs."

"Right." She nodded. "Among those positions, everyone is mostly equal, except for funeral directors. They take a lead role in both surface and interior professions."

"Why?"

"The funeral home is the centralized office where priors get their needs served. It's where they are assigned agents to help them finalize earthly issues, fill out paperwork, make preparations for their transfer, and it's also where the judicial system is housed. Funeral directors manage and maintain all sectors of AfterCorps for their region, so they are the leaders in both the surface and interior roles."

"You had me until the judicial system."

Sloane got out a blank piece of paper. "Let's take a look at the interior hierarchy; that'll help things make more sense for you."

"Okay." I felt pinpricks rise to goose bumps—the good kind, this time—when she started making the diagram, her arm grazing mine with each stroke of her pen.

"Here at the bottom are the clerks. They process paperwork and help priors fill it out as needed. Next are data organizers and analysts. Organizers gather information from people's lives and put together a report of all their big moments. Analysts determine what issues need to be worked out in this world before the dead can move on to the next."

"How do they get the data?"

Sloane shook her head. "I don't know. It's one of the things we're supposed to learn in training. Next up are the field agents. They work with both the priors and the currents to iron out those earthly affairs. They also advocate for priors when need be. They're kind of a social worker-attorney combo."

"But why would a ghost need an attorney?" The more she explained, the more confused I felt.

"Let me keep going, and you'll see." I had to admire her patience. She didn't seem even a little annoyed at all my interruptions. "Next up are the bounty hunters and the judges."

My eyes widened, but I kept my mouth shut.

"When misconduct occurs in life, people don't always get justice, and they almost never get justice that satisfies the leaders of the Cosworld."

"Cosworld is…"

"The afterlife, yeah. Cosmic world. So justice is distributed here so that priors can make their final transfer with a clean slate."

"Leaders of the cosmic world? So like…Zeus and Hades?"

"Nah, they're not gods, at least not the way you're thinking. They're more like heads of state. It's a bureaucratic system there, the same way it is here. Granted, there's a lot even our higher-ups don't know about what goes on over there. We learn enough to inform our procedures on this side, but there are plenty of details over there that are classified."

My mind swirled as I tried to absorb all of this. None of it was what I had pictured when I thought about the afterlife. Granted, I hadn't spent a ton of time thinking about it, but when I had, it had been visions of walking toward a bright light and stepping into a gauzy, magical place in the sky where dead spirits flew around and looked benevolently down on their loved ones on earth. Going from one bureaucratic world to another hadn't been in any of my imaginings, and it didn't sound that great.

"It's not what I expected when I learned about it either," Sloane said. I must have looked as shocked and confused as I felt. "We'll learn a lot more about it when classes start up again. *If* they start up again."

"Who created the hierarchy?"

"Well, ah, Myron Jasper did. Before AfterCorps, interpreters over the world had their own ways of assisting priors. There wasn't a large organization like this, but they did tend to gather in pockets and work in small groups. Part of what made Myron so great was that he spent years researching and conversing with interpreters from everywhere and took the best parts of what they did to form AfterCorps."

It amazed me the way her eyes glistened and hands gestured excitedly when she discussed AfterCorps's inception and history. I couldn't imagine getting so worked up over ghosts. Maybe if I'd learned all this back in middle school when I went through my ghost phase, but not now. I'd grown out of ghosts, or so I'd thought.

"Okay. So I guess the only thing left is the funeral directors, right? What are they called, managers?"

"Directors. Their title is basically the same in both areas. And there's one step between directors and the one we just discussed, which also brings us to your first question."

"Oh, right," I said. "What is the CDU?"

"The CDU is the Criminally Demonic Unit."

Chapter Twelve

Footsteps approaching from the living room stopped me from exploding in questions.

"Hey, Mom," Sloane said to the plump, dark-haired woman who entered the kitchen.

"Hey, babe." She turned to me. "Who's this?"

"Aria Jasper." I stood to shake her hand, and I saw something flicker across her eyes so quickly I couldn't tell what it was. Recognition at my last name? Caution? Fear? I couldn't even begin to guess why she'd be afraid that I was in her kitchen.

"Aria," she said and shook my hand. She smiled, and her eyes were warm, and whatever had been there before was replaced by cheerful friendliness. "I'm Sandy, nice to meet you. You kids aren't playing hooky, are you?"

"Training got canceled today," Sloane said, "so we thought we'd study together so we don't lose momentum."

"That's a sound idea. Why was training canceled?"

Sloane must have seen the pink in my cheeks. "I'll tell you about it later."

"All right," Sandy said after a thoughtful glance in my direction. "Aria, are you staying for dinner? I'm making meatball subs, Sloane's favorite."

I looked at my phone and saw that it was after five. My day with Sloane had flown by. "No, but thanks for the offer. It sounds terrific, but I should be getting home."

"Maybe some other time, then."

"I'm just going to walk Aria out." Sloane grabbed a pan from a high shelf for her mom. "Then I'll help you make dinner."

"Okay." Sandy smiled at me. "Come back and see us soon, Aria."

"I will." I couldn't help but smile back at her. "Thank you."

Sloane stepped onto the front porch and held the screen door for me, and we walked to my car together.

"Thank you for today, for everything," I said. "You're a good teacher."

"It was fun." She leaned against my car door and gave me a lazy smile. "Almost makes me hope training gets canceled tomorrow, too."

I wished I had agreed to stay for dinner, if only so it would be darker and my blush wouldn't be so obvious. Several moments of staring at each other went by. Finally, she broke the spell by turning and opening my car door and resting her arm on it as I approached the driver's seat.

"Have a good night," I murmured.

"Be careful driving home," she replied, and with those words, she put her other hand on my shoulder, and we were in each other's eyes again. I thought she was going to kiss me, and my lips parted a little. "See you tomorrow, Aria." Instead of kissing me, she tapped her forehead to mine, then took a small step back.

"See you." I got into my car. Halfway through my fifteen-minute drive, I reached up and touched my forehead where hers had been.

CHAPTER THIRTEEN

My parents were making dinner when I got home, and while they didn't seem exactly back to their old selves, it was the first time I'd seen them working together on anything since my birthday. Considering that they shared a business, a home, and an offspring, that was pretty huge, and it was a relief to see my mom setting the table and my dad flipping pork chops in the skillet.

"Hey, hon," Mom said. "Where've you been?"

"Studying at Sloane's," I said. To my father, "Ghost school was canceled today."

He nodded. "I know all about it, and we are going to remedy that problem tonight."

Before I could ask what that meant, my mom said, "Go and wash up for dinner. It'll be ready in just a few minutes."

"Okay."

I went upstairs to change clothes—nothing like pajama pants after a long day—and wash my hands. I stepped into the hallway, and in front of me was a crying Clara Braverman. I screeched. It was shocking to see anyone I wasn't expecting, but aside from that, Mrs. Braverman looked terrible. I couldn't see through her, and yet she was faded. The whites of her eyes were expanding, taking over half the irises, and she had a shiny appearance, as if she was clammy and covered in a slick layer of sweat.

"Mrs. Braverman? Clara? What's wrong?"

"You have to help me. You have to help me. They keep saying I'm not finished here, but I am. I am! I just want to leave this place, but they won't let me."

I reached out and was more surprised than I should've been that my fingers couldn't make contact. "Who won't let you?"

"Your father," she cried. "You have to convince him it's time to let me go."

"But...but why would my father keep you here?"

"He's a bad man." Clara nodded aggressively "He's spreading lies about me, and you've got to set it right."

"Aria?" My dad's voice floated up from the bottom of the stairs. "Dinner's getting cold."

And like someone had flipped a switch, Clara Braverman disappeared.

I looked through the rooms upstairs, calling out to her softly. She was gone, though, as quickly as she'd appeared. My heart pounded, and my entire body trembled. I slumped against the wall and wrapped my arms around my midsection as if holding myself tightly might help me get my shit together.

I couldn't remember the last time I'd been so scared. It had probably been when I was a child and had a nightmare. If only this was as simple as that had been. The nightmare had ended when I woke up, and my parents had rushed to my room, turned the light on, and comforted me until I felt safe again. This nightmare was happening while I was wide awake, and my parents were the ones keeping me in the dark.

❖

I was shaky as I descended the stairs, but by the time I got to the kitchen, I almost felt as if the incident with Mrs. Braverman hadn't even happened. Here in the warmth of the kitchen, when the gentle glow of candles lit the area around the table, and my parents had already heaped my plate with pork chops, mac and cheese, green beans, and a sourdough roll. There was even a glass of orange juice next to my plate.

I sat across from my mom and dad, looked at their smiling faces, and decided not to talk to them about Clara tonight. She was wrong or confused. Had to be.

"Dinner looks great," I said.

"Thanks," my parents said in unison and smiled at each other.

I had been worried about them. Worried about my mom, of course, but also worried about *them*. For the first time in a month, it was starting to feel as if things were going to be okay with my parents. I'd come home thinking I was going to confront them about all I'd learned earlier in the day, but they seemed so relaxed, and I didn't want to ruin that with questions about all the secrets they'd kept or whether my dad was some kind of monster.

I took a bite that was every bit as good as it looked and smelled.

"So," Dad said, "we've been quite remiss in telling you about AfterCorps and about your heritage."

My mouth was full, and I didn't really know what to say, so I nodded.

"We're going to fill you in on the basics tonight," she said.

I drank a swallow of orange juice. "Okay."

"You come from a long line of interpreters," my father said. "We can trace our lineage back nearly five hundred years. But more than about five generations back, it gets murky. We're going to focus on your great-great-grandfather and move forward."

"He's the one who wrote the textbook," I said.

"Yes, and he wrote many others. He is often called the father of modern interpretation. He founded Jasper Funeral Home and really pioneered the marriage of surface and interior careers so interpreters could make a living and have legitimacy while also having ready access to priors."

"He also created AfterCorps," Mom said. "It's evolved over

the years, but Myron organized all the facets of interpreters who had various skills and sects and gathered them into the central institution that AfterCorps is today."

"So before AfterCorps, interpreters were on their own?" I asked.

"There were small groups scattered all over the globe," he said. "And back then, it was a lot more difficult to connect people worldwide. Correspondence was slow and unreliable at best. But he made it his mission and his life's work to find the brightest interpreters in their areas of expertise and bring them on. Most of the interpreters he enrolled at AfterCorps have descendants still with us."

I took a moment to chew my mac and cheese and think. "So there are interpreters who aren't a part of AfterCorps?"

"Yes. Think of it like this: there are people who consider themselves spiritual, believing in one god or another, but not all of them go to the respective churches of their faiths. You can be a Christian and not belong to a church. You can be an interpreter and not belong to AfterCorps."

"But is that the choice of the individual interpreter or of AfterCorps when someone doesn't belong?"

"It varies," my mom said, and I thought I saw her smile fade a little.

"There's a lot to tell you," Dad said. "Your mother and I thought we were doing the right thing by keeping all of this from you. Our hope was that you wouldn't need any of this knowledge, but the truth is, we were wrong. You come from a family of proud leaders in interpretership, and this is your birthright."

"It's going take several years of training to find out what interior job you will have," my mom said. "But your dad and I think we've come up with a great option for a surface job."

"We certainly have," he said, beaming. "I think you'll find it a great compromise."

"Death singer," I said.

"Well," Mom said, "yes, although I don't think I'd call it

that." I could see she was remembering and regretting her old wedding singer joke. "How did you guess?"

"Sloane gave me a crash course on surface and interior jobs today. She was the one who guessed it. Looks like she was right."

"I know it's not a recording deal, honey," Dad said. "But you're going to be doing important, meaningful work for the rest of your life."

I looked at my mostly empty plate for a few moments. How could they both act as if this was something I could be happy about? Knowing what my life could have been and thinking that singing at funerals and escorting ghosts to run their final earthly errands could be any kind of substitute made me wonder if they even knew me at all. A horrible part of me even wished my mom would go back to her zombie state. At least then she had appeared as if she knew what I had lost and what that meant. "I think I'll go to my bedroom."

Mom and Dad looked at each other, their eyebrows lifted. Finally, he spoke. "If you could rinse your plate, I'd appreciate it. But we'll continue this conversation soon, Aria."

I dumped the last bits of food down the garbage disposal and stuck my plate in the dishwasher. When I went upstairs, I turned the hall light on, scared I might bump into Clara again, but it was empty. Now that I was by myself, it all seemed real again. *Great, I'm a twenty-two-year-old who's afraid of the dark.* I went to the bathroom and brushed my teeth, terrified with every movement and every step that the ghost might appear out of nowhere and start wailing about my father again.

I'd had the creeps about ghosts when I'd first found out I'd be able to interact with them, but since I'd only ever talked to Mrs. Braverman, and only at the funeral home, I'd relaxed into the knowledge that I could only communicate with them there. Tonight had proven me completely wrong, and now I felt robbed of all feelings of safety in my own home.

I went to my closet and pulled down a box of old things I'd outgrown. Underneath a battered old teddy bear, some pictures from my earliest recitals and a dried, crumbling corsage from a high school dance, I found what I was looking for: my old *Power Puff Girls* night-light. I plugged it in and was both delighted and relieved to see it still worked.

That night, I slept with a night-light for the first time since I was eight.

CHAPTER FOURTEEN

For the first time, I arrived at ghost school before Sloane. My sleep the night before had been tense and restless; every creak and groan of the house had woken me with a start, and I'd given up at seven and had gotten up. I looked at my phone now and saw it was almost fifteen minutes before nine o'clock. I was a little excited to see her.

I sat and got my notes and textbook out, then played on my phone. I frowned when I realized I'd missed a call from Macy the night before and sent her a text with a promise to call her tonight.

"Hey." Sloane strolled past me to her desk and sat. Today she wore a Led Zeppelin T-shirt, and I at least knew a few of their songs.

"Hey," I said and pointed at her shirt. "A band I've actually heard of."

She grinned. "Well, I would hope so. Led Zeppelin is some real music."

"After the song you played yesterday, I'm not sure if you're the best judge of real music," I said and was rewarded with a throaty laugh.

"Fair enough. Although I'm a little nostalgic about 'Alien Love'; my mom used to sing it to me in the morning when I was little, and she got me up for school. I don't necessarily think it would be my jam if it weren't for that."

"That's adorable," I said before I could stop myself.

"Thanks." Crooked smile.

"Good morning," came a booming voice. It wasn't Nick; it was my father. Immediately, I was on edge. It had become the norm for him to be uninvolved in my AfterCorps experience, and now that he was finally starting to be present, I should have been happy. I wondered why I wasn't.

"Nick will be along shortly, but I wanted to stop by this morning to welcome you. I try to get around and speak to new students during their first week of training and introduce myself." He smiled at me. "I'm already very acquainted with one of you, so why don't I focus on the interpreter-in-training to whom I've not been introduced?"

Sloane stood, and I noticed her hand was shaky when she reached to receive his handshake.

"I'm Nathan Jasper, and you are?"

"Sloane," she answered, her voice a little groggy. She cleared her throat and spoke again. "Sloane Dennison."

His smile widened. "You're Sandy Dennison's girl."

"That's right."

"Oh, I've known Sandy for years; she was only a few years behind me in training."

"Yes. She speaks very highly of you, sir."

He waved. "Oh, please don't bother with any sir business. You can call me Nathan." When Sloane shook her head, he laughed so loudly it echoed against the cinder block walls. "Or maybe you can start by calling me Mr. Jasper. Would that make you more comfortable?"

"It would, Mr. Jasper."

"Very fine, very fine. Tell me, Sloane, what do you aspire to do as part of the AfterCorps organization?"

"I…I'm interested in being a part of the CDU."

He stole a quick glance at me before turning back to her. "That's quite a tough division. I like a student with lofty goals."

A shiver tickled the base of my spine. The longer he stood

before us, the more uncomfortable I became. In the past, I would have said that he was the most authentic human being I knew, so why did all of this feel like a forced, disingenuous charade?

Nick arrived, nodded at my father, and went to his desk. He started taking things out of his bag.

"Well, I see your fearless leader is here." Dad handed Sloane a business card. "Please know that I'm only a text or call away should you have anything you'd like to discuss. That's an open offer." He smiled at her, leaned in to give me a quick hug, and waved at Nick on his way out. Nick gave him a slight nod again.

Nick had always been my dad's right-hand man and one of his closest friends. It was odd to see him being so curt. I wondered how their talk had gone yesterday. But my parents had given me the beginning of a rundown on our family history last night, and ghost school was open again, so things had to be better.

After pulling the last item—a green pear—out of his bag, Nick walked to the front of his desk, sat on it, and studied us.

"How did your studying go yesterday?" He shined the pear on his checkered shirt and took a bite. "Did you both read the first chapters?"

I nodded and glanced at Sloane, who did the same.

"What did you think?"

"It was sort of an overview of stuff I already knew," Sloane said.

"And you, Aria?" He asked around another bite of pear. "You've had less of a chance to acquaint yourself with interpretership in the past."

"Actually, Sloane and I did some studying together yesterday after you..." I stumbled over my words. "After training was canceled. She went over the basics of the hierarchy with me, so I wasn't completely unprepared when I got to our homework."

He lifted an eyebrow. "Going above and beyond for the director's daughter isn't a bad strategy, Sloane. It won't get you into CDU, but it can't hurt. Now..."

But I didn't hear what he said for several moments after that.

Was that what she was doing? Sucking up to the main dude's daughter? I felt like a bucket of ice water had been dropped on me.

"Aria?"

"What?"

He was standing at the blackboard and had written "Discussion Questions" on it. "What questions do you have after what you read yesterday?"

It took me a second to get out of my head and open my notes. I looked at my hurried handwriting and tried to find a question. "I guess one of the first things I'd like to know is, how can you tell when someone is a prior? I know none of us could tell at the time of our quickening."

"It's something you learn to distinguish as you start to work with them," he said. "For one thing, you learn to sense the slight drop in temperature."

I thought of all the times I'd watched horror movies where people started shivering when a ghost was around. "That's a real thing?"

"Yes, but it's more subtle than you think unless a ghost is agitated."

I was cold last night when I was in the hallway with Mrs. Braverman, but the reason hadn't occurred to me. "Okay. What else?"

Nick paused. "You start to develop a…a sort of Spidey sense about it. Before you know that someone near you is a prior, it's easy to think they're a reg. But now that you know, you'll be able to identify them more and more. The energy in the room shifts when you're talking to a ghost. The air feels more stagnant, almost dry. It's easier to identify them in the summer, which is part of the reason that we always begin training in June. Our Ohio summers lend humidity and heat, which helps us to distinguish when that cool papery feeling appears in the air."

"So we don't use K2 meters or EVP recorders to help identify them?" Sloane asked.

Nick frowned. "Where did you hear about those kinds of things?"

She grinned. "I have done more research than you can imagine while I waited for my formal training to start. Especially when I thought I might not get to take classes."

"I see. No, we don't use tools that regs commonly use for their 'ghost hunting' sessions." He scrunched his nose. "The people who resort to those contraptions do so because they wish they had the kinds of gifts we have, and for the most part, they're hacks and charlatans."

I couldn't understand why any reg would want to run around trying to chase ghosts if they didn't have to. They could do whatever they wanted with their lives, unlike me, and they chose to hunt for stray spirits? Regs had no idea how lucky they were.

"Other questions?" He scrawled some bullet points from our discussion on the chalkboard.

"What do we do if a ghost comes to us when we're not in training?" I asked.

He frowned again, and this time, there were deep lines carved into his forehead. "What do you mean?"

"I mean...now that we've had our quickening, ghosts might start approaching us, right? What are we supposed to do if that happens, say, when we're alone?"

Halfway through my question, he was shaking his head. "I think I know what you're talking about, Aria, and you don't have to worry about it. Mrs. Braverman, right?"

How did he know? "Uh, yeah."

"The day she met you in the funeral home, your father and I were right outside the door, a few feet away. The only reason she was able to communicate with you directly was because two established interpreters were so near."

"Really? How close does an established interpreter have to be in order for there to be...contact?"

"Very close, no farther than a room away or maybe twenty feet."

My father had definitely been farther than that when I was upstairs; he was all the way down in the kitchen, but I didn't press it. I didn't like the look of those lines on Nick's forehead.

"This is a good time to discuss what we'll be doing tomorrow," he said. "Since it will be the beginning of your hands-on training. We'll be going to the other side of the basement tomorrow, taking the official tour."

"I knew there had to be more to this place than a conference room," I said.

"Indeed. There's an entire area on the other side of Sally's desk where priors are assigned a clerk and a field agent, the hearing room for judicial proceedings, and the transfer room. We'll be touring the entire thing to give you a feel for the workings of AfterCorps."

"Do priors live here?" I paused when I realized my poor choice of wording. "I mean, is this where they stay?"

"No, they come here for their meetings and appointments. Other than that, they're free to wander as they see fit."

No kidding.

"Nick, do all funeral homes have AfterCorps centers like this?" Sloane asked.

He returned to the chalkboard. "Excellent question. Not all funeral homes are affiliated with AfterCorps. Sometimes, a funeral home is just a funeral home. And of all the affiliates, they all have centers for clerk and field agents, but only one mortuary in every state houses special divisions such as judiciary, transfers, CDU, etc."

"Is it always in the state capital?" she asked.

"Yes. Very good." He began making another list. "Things to remember for tomorrow: it seems counterintuitive, but you'll be leaving your notebooks and pens at home. You'll be observing, but we don't want to be taking notes and making priors feel like science experiments. That's not conducive to any of our processes. I'll give you notes afterward that summarize what you should have seen and learned. Secondly, you'll want to bring a jacket. The change in temperature is subtle when you're dealing with one prior, but it's significant when there are several of them, especially when you're still getting used to it. Thirdly, you'll have minimal interaction with priors. If they approach you, be polite, but don't start or extend conversations. That's not what tomorrow is for, and I'll be there to intervene if they try to engage with you."

"Are we going to be seeing the CDU division tomorrow?" Sloane sounded eager.

His face tightened. "No. CDU hearings are held here, but I made sure we weren't going when one of those was on the docket. And the division itself is…elsewhere, for safety."

"Whose safety?" she asked.

The clench in his jaw was unmistakable this time. "Everyone's."

CHAPTER FIFTEEN

H ey, Aria, wait up!"
I had hurried out of the classroom and half jogged to my car, and Sloane was running after me, out of breath by the time she reached my door.

I let her catch her breath and didn't say a word. Nick's words about her sucking up to the boss's daughter echoed through my thoughts. I felt foolish and embarrassed that I'd allowed myself to fall for what I'd thought had been her interest in me.

"Did you want to study together some before you go home?" She pulled her phone out of her pocket and checked the time. "It's only three o'clock."

"Nah, I should go."

She touched my elbow, and I hated the feeling of heat blooming on my cheeks. "Hey, what's wrong?"

"Nothing, I just…I just don't want you to feel like you have to be super nice to me because of who my family is."

She laughed a little until I pulled away. "Aria, do you honestly think that's why I'm spending time with you?"

I shrugged. "I mean, I don't know you that well. It might be." I didn't want her to see that I was hurt, so I kept my face carefully neutral.

"Well, it's not."

"Okay." I wanted her to be telling the truth. "You tell me, then. What do you get out of tutoring someone who knows next to nothing about all of this when you have obviously made it a huge part of your life?"

She leaned on my car in that casual way she had. So far, she'd looked comfortable and at home everywhere. "For one thing, you and I are starting our training together, which means we will be spending a lot of time together over the next three years. There's a good chance our class size will always be two, and it would be nice if we could be study buddies who help each other get through it."

I wilted a little inside. Of course it was for practical reasons that she wanted to spend time together, and not because of any interest in me. She'd been ready to practice interpretership for so long that she'd probably take whatever study partner she could get. "Makes sense. And for another thing?"

"For another thing," she said, leaning forward and resting a hand on my waist. "I think you're funny and interesting, and you have the greenest eyes I've ever seen. Is that a good enough reason to want to get to know you?"

I tried to form words, but all I could do was nod. My heart, wilted in my chest just a moment earlier, now felt as if it was alive for the first time. The blood pulsated through my body with a force I hadn't known before.

"Good." She smiled. "So do you want to study?"

"I do, honestly, but I haven't seen my best friend in days. I was going to invite her over for a while this afternoon so she doesn't feel like I've abandoned her for ghosts. How about tomorrow, after our big tour?"

"Does your father know you told a reg about the ghosts?" She arched an eyebrow.

"No. And after all the ways he's lied to me over the years, I don't feel even remotely bad about it. Besides, I trust Macy. We've kept each other's secrets since we were five, and I know she won't breathe a word to anyone."

"Well, that's good enough for me." I loved the way her smiie crept across her face so slowly, as if she never had a worry in the world.

"Anyway, how about tomorrow?"

"I'll hold you to it."

❖

"Oh my God, tell it to me again!" Macy nearly shrieked.

We were in the basement with a bowl of popcorn between us. *Gingerdead Man* was playing on TV, but Macy had muted it when I started telling her about Sloane.

"The story isn't going to change," I told her, but I couldn't help laughing.

Macy had pulled up Sloane's Instagram page and squealed at how adorable she was. "At least one of us has a love interest this summer," she said and tossed a handful of popcorn in her mouth.

"No cute guys at the pool?"

Macy had gotten a position as a lifeguard to hold her over until she found her first grown-up job. "More like toddlers in poopy swim diapers."

"Gross," I said, but I couldn't help laughing.

"You know, I've really missed you. It's weird spending all this time apart and not knowing what's going on with you."

"I know. I'm sorry."

"So, new crush aside, how's it all going?"

I put a handful of popcorn in my mouth to give myself a moment to think. I didn't know how much I should even share with Macy, a fact that made me uncomfortable since I'd always told her everything. If there were rules about how much or little to tell a reg, I hadn't learned them yet, and my father had no one to blame but himself if I said something I shouldn't. My initial reaction to spill everything had subsided, leaving me unsure how to proceed.

"It's nothing like I expected," I said. "You and I have watched every horror film we could get our hands on, and none of this seems similar to when people talk to ghosts in movies." I paused. "Except the whole feeling cold when there's a ghost around."

"Have you seen more ghosts?" Her eyes were wide, and she gripped the edge of the popcorn bowl.

"Yeah, one."

"What was it like?"

"A little scary. She's waiting for her final transfer, and there have been some complications with it. She's understandably upset, but hopefully, it'll all get worked out soon." I decided not to tell her what Clara said about my father, mostly because I still didn't know what to make of it.

"*Final transfer*," she screeched. "Is that what you call it?"

I shrugged. I was ready to talk about something else. Not only had I just lied to her for the first time, I was becoming bothered by how fascinated she was with the novelty of all this and knew this was why there was so much secrecy surrounding AfterCorps and what they did. If things had been reversed, I'd want her to spill all the secrets about ghosts too. It was natural, but it made me uncomfortable, in large part because it made me confront how very little I knew about what was going on in my own life.

"We have to call it something," I replied.

Macy knew me well. She stared at me for several seconds. "I'm sorry. This has to be hard enough without me freaking out about everything you tell me."

"It's…" I felt as if I was going to cry. "It's not what I had planned for my life."

"I know."

"And it's scary, you know? These are scary things I'm dealing with, and I feel so unprotected. I can't believe my parents let me be so vulnerable all this time and even now. Since my quickening, they've barely told me anything. I'm dealing with ghosts now, the time for secrecy is clearly over, but they still are keeping me in the dark."

"I can't even imagine how hard that must be. There has to be a way to get them to open up to you about it."

"Yeah. I need to figure something out." I grabbed the remote and turned the volume up on *Gingerdead Man*. "Enough about me. Let's watch our movie. I'm dying to see what happens."

"Pun intended?" Macy grinned.

"You know it."

❖

I walked upstairs after Macy left that night, and on the way to my bedroom, my dad called me in. He and Mom were sitting up in bed with books in their laps. She was reading *Hem* by Octavia Reese, and he was rereading *Great Expectations* for what had to be the two hundredth time.

"Aria," Dad said, taking his glasses off. "I wanted to talk to you a little bit about tomorrow."

"About the tour?"

"Ah." He cleared his throat and glanced at Mom. "No. I needed to talk to you about what's happening after the tour."

"Okay...what's happening?" I had an idea of what he was going to say, and dread, thick and dark, filled my lungs. I took shallow breaths to keep from choking on it.

"We don't usually worry about adding surface duties to training until after students have completed their first year, but since you are already trained in that area..."

"You want me to sing at a funeral tomorrow?"

"It was my idea," my mom said. "I don't want you to get rusty."

A squashed laugh escaped my mouth. This was the last thing I wanted to do. The inky dread threaded through my body and settled in my stomach. "What difference does it make if I get rusty? I'm not going to be a performer, not the kind I wanted to be. And I've heard enough singers at funerals to know the bar is set pretty low as far as quality goes."

"Aria!" Dad slammed his book closed. "I understand that this is a dramatic change for you, and we are going above and beyond to be sensitive about your feelings. But you need to recognize the tremendous honor and gift that has been afforded to you. The extraordinary life you had planned will one day pale in comparison to the opportunity you now have."

Mom slid her hand up and down Dad's forearm, and his breathing slowed back to a normal rate. I crossed my arms and pinched my lips together, glaring. I couldn't think of anything I'd rather do less than become a death singer. In that moment, I felt as if, given the choice between death singer and never singing again, I'd choose the latter.

"Give it a chance, Aria," my mom said quietly.

"I don't really have a choice, do I?"

"Only in your attitude." Mom let that hang in the air for a moment. "I'll meet you at the funeral home at three o'clock tomorrow so we can practice. I'll be playing the piano during the funeral, so I have the sheet music all set."

"What will I be singing?"

"'Amazing Grace,'" Dad said.

"Fine," I said. "Is that all?"

They nodded, and I turned and left.

Back in my own room, I stretched out on the bed, my mind racing and my heart pounding. I thought of all the times I'd wanted to run away since getting this news and wondered why I hadn't looked into it beyond a lovely fantasy. I grabbed my phone from my nightstand and pulled up the Greyhound Bus website. There was a bus leaving for Los Angeles in three days. I clicked the field for a one-way ticket, and before I had time to change my mind, I hit purchase. I was done being a bystander in my own life and decided it was time for me to be in charge of what was happening to me. For the first time in weeks, I got a sound night's sleep.

CHAPTER SIXTEEN

I knew I needed to keep going to ghost school until I made my getaway so as not to raise suspicion. It was funny how I didn't mind driving to the funeral home that morning, knowing it would be one of three more days I'd have to do it. I even found myself humming along with the radio and was startled by the realization that I'd barely sung at all since my birthday.

My first impression of the other offices in AfterCorps was that they were a lot more like the bureau of motor vehicles than I expected. Sloane and I stood near the entrance with Nick and looked around. Rows of hard, uncomfortable-looking chairs filled the center, and several bored-looking priors filled some of the chairs. A tall counter made an L-shape on one end of the room, and interpreters stood behind it. Above the counters a digital screen had a number on it, and each time the number went up, one of the interpreters called a new prior to the counter. Like my recent experience at the BMV when I renewed my driver's license, it was freezing. I wrapped my cardigan tightly around me and tied the belt.

"Number thirty-three," called a woman whose curly blond hair was crunchy with gel. "Thirty-three to window two."

A beautiful young woman with a tall afro walked to the window, and the two began conversing over some paperwork.

"This is the beginning stage for priors," Nick said. "Here,

they start the process of the transfer. That young lady is receiving information regarding her life data as well as her assignment to a field agent."

I noticed Sloane giving a quick wave to someone and saw her mom behind the counter at window five. Mrs. Dennison smiled and gave a short nod before turning back to the prior at her station.

"Clerks are our front-line people. They're usually the first interpreter a prior meets, so they have to be great at making a strong first impression and putting them at ease, which is not always easy to do."

"How do the priors get here?" I asked. "After they die, I mean…how do they know to come to AfterCorps?"

"That's part of the reason funeral homes are the perfect location to house AfterCorps," he said. "We'll cover it more in our next class, but ghosts come to the site where the ceremony to acknowledge their death takes place. That's why, in every culture, as far back as the beginning of time, there have been rituals to honor the dead."

"But not every person who dies gets a funeral," Sloane said. "And not every funeral happens in a funeral home."

"You're right. We have provisions for those situations. Let's have that discussion in class tomorrow."

I had a moment of wishing I'd been able to bring my notebook before remembering I wouldn't need to learn any of this stuff.

"Let's step over here." He gestured to a wall opposite the counters, which had around a dozen doors. We went into a room so tiny, it felt stifling with three of us in it. It had a small desk with a chair on either side.

"This is where priors have their first meetings with a field agent," Nick said. "After they get the file from the clerk, they're given their appointment time, and they return here. We have several safe zones where they can wait in the meantime, as they begin to formulate their personal goals for the end of their time on earth. They build their transfer plan with their agent and discuss what life items need to be completed and how best to do that."

"What kinds of life items are we talking about?" Sloane asked.

"By and large, it's stuff like making sure a will is carried out the way they'd like or getting messages to loved ones. We have to do this in ways that make their friends and family feel as if they've stumbled across the messages so they don't discover our organization. If there have been any family estrangements, they often want to plant some seeds to reunify people, and we facilitate that as well."

He led us out and down a few doors to one that was slightly open. He gently pushed it open and motioned for us to come closer. Sloane and I shared space, standing so close our arms pressed together. I pulled my arm across my body. The only thing I'd miss about AfterCorps was this closeness with Sloane, and I wanted to distance myself from her so it wouldn't be so difficult to leave her behind. Of course, I felt pretty bad that my leaving would probably mean the end of ghost training for her. I hoped she would understand that I was only doing what I had to do.

The agent behind the desk gave a split-second glance in our direction before turning back to the prior. He was a broad-backed man with salt and pepper hair, and he held a picture in front of the agent. "I brought that doll back from New York for Rebecca. I was on my way to give it to her when…"

The agent took the picture and made some notes in a small notebook, the kind I'd seen police officers use. "I understand, Mr. Studebaker," she said. "We'll work on making sure the doll gets to the little girl." She handed the picture back and picked up a sheet of paper from a file on the desk. "Now, we need to get to the business of a disagreement you had with your sister, Cathy."

Nick pulled the door so it was only open an inch. He began walking toward the grand doorway at back of the room, talking softly as we followed him.

"In the next several months, you'll have the opportunity

to shadow clerks and field agents as they go about their work. In fact, as part of your training, you'll be working with several interpreters at different levels. It's key in establishing what your interests and strengths are, and it is vital to understand the big picture of how things happen at AfterCorps, regardless of what job you have."

We arrived at a marble archway that was so grand and luxurious, it looked completely out of place in the drab room. Mahogany double doors with wrought iron handles stood directly ahead of us, and off to the side stood an ancient, tiny man with the thickest glasses I'd ever seen. His eyes looked huge, like an owl's, and I wondered how big they were when he took his specs off. He stood behind a podium with a stack of papers on it.

"Nick!" he yelled and stepped out to shake Nick's hand. "We haven't seen you down here in a while."

Nick smiled and shook his hand. I noticed how gently he held it, as if afraid it might shatter in his large, mitt-like palm. "Good to see you, Bernard. I'm here with some new trainees." He gestured to us. "Meet Sloane Dennison and Aria Jasper."

Sloane and I rushed over to Bernard when he began to hobble over to us.

"I'm Aria," I said when he shook my hand.

"Sloane."

Bernard's eyes got somehow even bigger when he shook Sloane's hand. "You're Sandy's daughter. I've seen many pictures of you over the years." He smiled. "Sandy is always a love."

"Thank you," she said and flashed her crooked smile.

"Bernard, I'm showing these young people around today. We'd like to see some court proceedings while we're here."

"Certainly," he said. "Go on in; things should just be getting started."

"Thank you." Nick opened the door on the right. When I saw the level of effort it took for him to pull the door wide enough for us to get through, I wondered if I'd be able to open it myself.

More of those hard chairs formed rows in the courtroom,

and half a dozen people sat in them. We followed Nick to a set of stairs on the left and went up to a small balcony. We had just sat on a long bench that reminded me of a church pew when a voice said, "All rise."

We stood and saw a tall woman with deep dark skin and silvery gray hair step out and into the judge's seat. Unlike judges I'd seen on TV, she wore a bright blue robe. The bailiff, who wore a bright blue suit, continued:

"The honorable Judge Vivica Jenkins presides over hearings on this day, the twenty-first of June."

"Thank you, Paul," Judge Jenkins said. "Who is first on the docket today?"

"A Mr. Jack Dugan and his representative, Agent Striker."

"Mr. Dugan, Agent Striker, please step forward." She took a file from the bailiff and leafed through it.

A man with a black leather jacket and shiny dark hair stepped forward to the table facing the judge, and an older, stocky man in a beige shirt and jeans stood beside him.

"Good morning," Judge Jenkins said. "Mr. Dugan, I see you were charged with four counts of first-degree emotional embezzlement and have performed fifteen hundred hours of dominion service, is that correct?"

"Yes, Your Honor," Jack said.

"Agent Striker, have you found that Mr. Dugan has successfully and in good faith completed his dominion service to the extent that retribution has been served?" The judge paged through the file, not looking up.

"I have, Your Honor," said Agent Striker.

"In that case, Mr. Dugan, I recommend to the board of relegation that you be approved for your final transfer as quickly as it can be arranged."

Jack Dugan burst into tears. "Oh, thank you, Your Honor."

The emotion coming from the ghost was raw and palpable. I was startled to find tears fill my own eyes, and I blinked to keep them from falling. I'd never been a sympathetic cryer in the past, and it shocked me that I was overcome with emotions for this stranger. A quick glance at Sloane and Nick confirmed that neither of them were struggling with any tears.

The judge did look up then and nodded at him. "Safe travels, sir." She handed the file back to the bailiff. "Next case, Paul?"

Nick stood and motioned for us to follow. We went down the steps and back to the mahogany doors. We filed out in a single line, and as we did, Agent Striker escorted Jack through the doors beside us. The prior brushed against me when he passed, and I felt stabbing pain in my head, like the worst brain freeze I'd ever had. I stopped short, grasped my head. and caused Sloane to bump into me.

"Aria, are you okay?" Her hands were on my shoulders, guiding me forward. I kept my eyes closed and let her push me through the doors.

"What's wrong?" Nick asked.

"I don't know," Sloane said. They sounded really far away.

I crouched, my fingers interlaced over my scalp, waiting for the searing pain to subside. Never had I felt pain like this in my life, and I was scared. It felt as if I would die if it didn't start to fade away, and I began to panic. Finally, when I was beginning to think it would never end, it did. It only lasted a minute or two, but it felt like the longest moments of my life.

When I opened my eyes, Sloane crouched in front of me, and Nick bent at the waist, both looking at me with concern.

"That was the strangest thing," I said. "He bumped me and then my head…"

"Phantom frost," Nick said.

"What is that?" Sloane rested her hand on my knee.

"Sometimes, being touched by a prior, particularly one who has been here a long time before their transfer, causes that kind of pain. The longer they're here, the colder the air around them feels. Phantom frost indicates a sensitivity to the breakdown ghosts go through when they are earthbound for a long time."

"Will it stop happening?" I asked. "When I'm not so new to this?"

"Not exactly," he said. "But you build up a tolerance to it."

Great.

"Are you okay to stand?" Sloane asked.

"I think so." I took her outstretched hands and let her help me back into an upright position. I felt unsteady and disoriented, and focused on the feel of the solid marble floor under my feet and the warmth of Sloane's hands around mine.

"Are you two ready for the last stop on the tour?" Nick asked.

Sloane looked at me. "Are we?"

I'd never felt less ready for anything, but I did want to get this over with. "Onward and upward."

❖

It turned out that we actually went downward. We went down a little corridor past the mahogany doors, and at the end of it stood an elevator. Nick pushed the down button, and the doors opened. The three of us stepped on and began a rapid descent. I couldn't tell if my stomach was uneasy because of the speedy elevator or from nerves. My head still throbbed with a dull ache after my brush with the ghost, and who knew what possibly painful experiences awaited me where we were going? Moments later, we stepped out into a room whose walls, floor, and ceiling were made of shiny black granite.

"This is a little ominous," I said.

"Granite is the perfect material for helping priors travel to their final destination," Nick explained. "Lessons on that to come in future classes." He spoke quietly, but his words bounced off every surface and echoed. "This way."

A man in a bright blue robe like the one the judge wore stood at the opposite end of the room. The single light in this cavernous space came from a little alcove filled with blinding white light a few feet from where he stood.

"Who is it?" asked the man in the robe.

"It's me, Edgar," Nick said. We walked closer, and Nick turned to us. "Don't look directly into the light."

"Ah, Nick. Who do you have with you?"

"Aria Jasper and Sloane Dennison," he said. "My new students. Aria, Sloane, this is Edgar Blevins. He's been the Chief Officer of Transfers for nearly fifty years now."

"Fifty years come August." Edgar smiled. I was close enough to see that his eyes were the color of snow: white with a pale blue shift. It took me a few moments to understand that he was blind.

"Nice to meet you," I said.

Edgar walked toward my voice, his hand outstretched. I glanced at Nick, and he gave a curt nod. I wasn't sure how to interpret that, so I simply let the blind man rest his hand on my forehead when he reached me.

"Aria Jasper," he said. "Great, great-granddaughter of Myron Jasper, the founder of modern interpretation. Powerful skills are within you, more powerful, even, than your father. You come from two lines of extraordinarily gifted interpreters, and if you are able to harness your talents, you will be unstoppable."

He removed his hand, and I realized the warmth of it had removed the final lingering of my phantom frost headache. Could I truly be as powerful as that? In the months since finding out I could see ghosts, I'd felt everything from devastation to horror, but I'd never once felt extraordinary or talented. I would have recognized those untapped talents in myself by now, if they were there. And yet…if I was honest with myself, I hadn't given myself a chance to recognize anything other than my unwillingness to participate in this new way of life.

"Sloane Dennison," Edgar said, placing his palm on her forehead. "Ambition burns within you. Ambition and a great desire for adventure and justice. You have a warrior's spirit that, I daresay, is only equaled in your teacher."

He took a few steps back. "Be wary as you start your life of service to AfterCorps. Your strengths are also your weaknesses, never truer than when working with the dead. To find your true calling within our fine organization, you must first shed your expectations. What you desire may not be your calling, and in the end, we must always remember that we are here to serve the dead as we will one day want to be served by the living: with honor and dignity and the yearning to send these people forward to the place where they can live once again."

His speech echoed and repeated, allowing us to hear every word several times over. Minutes seemed to go by before the chamber was silent again. I felt every word as they seemed to bounce onto me. I had been raised among a lot of discussions about death and what it meant for the people still living, but my parents hadn't talked much about their views of the afterlife. On the rare occasions I had talked to them about it, they'd said I would form my own opinions on the subject when I got older. I had always sort of thought that death was the end, and now I had learned it was a beginning. A million questions flew through my mind about what it meant for the dead to live again. The gravity of the realization felt like an anvil on my chest, and for the hundredth time, I wondered how my parents could have kept me so in the dark.

"Thank you for your time, Edgar." Nick turned to us and tipped his head in Edgar's direction.

"Thank you," Sloane and I chorused.

Edgar gave a small bow, then turned away and shuffled back to stand sentry at the blinding alcove.

Nick herded us to the elevator, pressed the up arrow, and we got on.

"Was he blind before he became Chief Officer of Transfers, or was that an occupational hazard?" Sloane asked.

"The COT must give up his or her sight when they are appointed to the job," Nick said as the elevator doors opened.

"What?" I asked.

"He is with every prior when the transfer occurs, but we are not allowed to see what happens when the transfer takes place. It's one of our most stringent decrees that must never be broken. Even in the death work we do, there are very few things we know about what happens in the next destination. Some of our ancient predecessors did learn quite a bit about the Cosworld when they were establishing the primitive ways of interpretership, and many of them suffered greatly from it."

"Suffered in what way?" I asked.

"Madness, mostly. We've discussed a bit of what happens to priors if they remain on earth too long; it breaks them down mentally, emotionally, and physically, being in a world in which they don't belong. That goes both ways. We are not meant to know the in-depth goings on of the Cosworld, and so we protect that with all of our resources."

What must it have been like for interpreters hundreds or even thousands of years ago? Having to figure out the needs of ghosts through trial and error sounded absolutely dreadful. I'd felt so lost trying to acclimate myself to being an interpreter, but I couldn't imagine having to start from scratch with no help from anyone. How lonely and scary that must have been.

We walked through the beige open area we'd first come in through and out to the waiting area for AfterCorps.

"Nick," I said, "why did Edgar say I come from two lines of interpreters? Did two lines merge into one at some point?"

He nodded. "Something like that. Although your father would be the one who could give you more information about your lineage." Annoyance and anger bubbled in my stomach at the thought of asking my father anything. Would he tell me the truth? Would he tell me anything at all? The breakdown of my relationship with my parents was a wound that continued to grow, with no sign of healing. It was a big part of the reason I was so ready to run away from all of this. Not only had I been catapulted into this world I'd known nothing about, but my mom and dad had barely given me any explanation about all of it. I felt so alone, and I wanted to escape that feeling almost as much as I wanted to run from my responsibilities to AfterCorps.

We reached the top of the stairs in the back hallway of the funeral home and stepped outside into the muggy day.

"It's a little after two-thirty," Nick said. "I think this is a good time to stop. I have some surface funeral business I need to take care of this afternoon. See you both in the morning." He looked into the sky and inhaled deeply, then turned and went back inside.

"So," Sloane said, "if I remember correctly, we have a study date this afternoon."

"Oh, uh…"

"You're not canceling on me, are you?"

"I don't want to," I said, and nothing had ever been truer. "But it turns out I have some death singer duties this afternoon. Probably the same funeral Nick has to tend to."

"Really?" Sloane asked. "I didn't think our surface duties were supposed to start until we were a year or two into the program."

"Yeah. I guess, since I'm already trained on my surface job, they want me to get started sooner."

She tipped her head to the side. "Can I watch?"

I laughed. "The funeral is probably going to last at least an hour, and my song will only be about three minutes long. Trust me, you don't wanna hang around for this." I saw my mom pull up in the parking lot. "Anyway, my mom is here, and we're going to practice for a bit before the funeral starts. I'll see you tomorrow, okay?"

"Sure." She completely surprised me by leaning in and giving me a kiss on the cheek. "See you tomorrow." When she turned, I pressed my hand to my cheek.

It felt stupid to want to rearrange my plans, give up on my dreams, and stay somewhere I didn't want to be, all because of the heat I felt from a kiss by a girl I'd known for only a few days. I frowned and thought about that. It wasn't exactly true that I was having second thoughts only because of Sloane. I'd been having mixed feelings since being in the depths of AfterCorps with Edgar. Somehow, those few minutes with him had been more meaningful to me than any other conversations I'd had about being an interpreter.

Mom crossed the parking lot to me, and I had to set my thoughts aside. "Who was that?" she asked.

"Sloane. My classmate."

She studied me. "Just your classmate?"

"I hope not. We'll see."

She opened the door, and I walked inside and followed her to the practice room.

I'd sung "Amazing Grace" more times than I could count, so the practice was mostly getting me warmed up and telling me where I'd sit during the service and where I'd stand when it was time to sing.

Shortly before the funeral started, Mom and I went into the large parlor and took our places. She sat at the piano and began to play the opening hymn, and I sat in a folding chair just behind her. The last time I performed, it was in a venue with nearly a thousand people; now here I was, a death singer.

A young woman walked past, her sobs muffled by the tissue she held over her mouth. A wave of guilt washed over me as I realized I'd been about to enter yet another reverie, lamenting all I had lost, when I was surrounded by people who'd lost someone they loved. I made the decision to be present for this funeral and do my best for the people who'd come to say good-bye.

About three-quarters of the way through the service, it was time. I stood to the side and just in front of the piano, and as my mom began to play, the lights dimmed and a slideshow of the deceased played on the screen behind the casket. I began to sing, and even though it was in a dark room behind a bunch of mourners instead of in the spotlight onstage in front of hundreds or thousands of people, the same thing happened that had happened every time I sang. My blood pulsed through my body, and I had goose bumps all over. My voice, strong and clear, filled the room, and I felt alive. When I finished, it was to the sound of loud sniffles and people blowing their noses rather than applause. I sat and nodded at a few people who looked over their shoulders to smile and mouth, "Thank you."

I'd wondered whether the prior was in attendance and had been scanning the room for her since I sat. I saw no sign. Over to the left, something in the doorway caught my eye, and when the lights came back up, I saw Sloane leaning there, resting her head on the door frame. She smiled and mimed clapping. I was overwhelmed at how glad I was to see her and how happy it made me that she hadn't listened when I told her not to stay. My heart felt too big for my chest, as if it expanded to make room for this sudden rush of giddiness.

A few minutes later, when I looked back, she was gone. I went home, and while I sat at the table eating an apple, I pulled my phone out and saw a text from her.

Your voice is heaven.

I typed a thank-you and hugged myself. I realized that she was becoming more than just a crush. I cared about her, and I thought she cared about me too. My phone vibrated, and I picked it up, expecting to see another text, but instead found a confirmation from Greyhound with an itinerary for my trip in two days. Not for the first time that day, I had doubts about my plans to leave. California held all my dreams, everything I'd worked for my whole life. Columbus held death. That was what I'd thought when I bought my ticket. The events of today made me realize it wasn't that simple, and now I didn't know what I was going to do.

CHAPTER SEVENTEEN

I woke up shivering before my alarm went off the next morning and lay in bed, letting my eyes adjust to the early morning darkness. At some point in the night, I'd kicked my blanket to the floor. When I reached to grab it, my eyes went to a pair of shoes in the corner that weren't mine. I rubbed my eyes and squinted; the shoes were attached to a person. I tried to scream but could only let out gasping breaths.

Mrs. Braverman stepped out of the shadows, and I snatched my blanket from the floor and wrapped it around me. Terror gripped me with icy fingers, and I shook even as I scrambled toward the head of my bed. I tried to tell myself she couldn't hurt me and to stay calm, but I was anything but calm. A ghost in my room was worse than any nightmare I'd ever had.

"I tried to wait until you were awake. I must speak to you." She sat on the edge of my bed, and I pulled the blanket more tightly around my shoulders.

"My transfer keeps getting delayed," she said. "It's not right. I didn't do what they said I did. I didn't do it." Her voice was hoarse like mine got when I hadn't gotten enough sleep.

"What do they say you did?" I asked, fighting to keep my teeth from chattering. "And who is they?"

"They say I murdered my husband," she whispered. "Sol died of a heart attack. I had an autopsy performed because it happened so suddenly." She took a shaky breath, and I started thinking about why ghosts would need to breathe at all. "You don't know the things they're making me do for my dominion service. Simply horrifying."

"Clara, I'm so, so sorry you're going through this, but I don't know what I would even be able to do for you. I'm less than a week into my training. I'm just barely getting into the basics of what all this is about. I don't have the power or knowledge to help you. Maybe my father—"

"No!" She grasped my wrist, and a surge of pain flowed from my spine up into my brain. I cried out and grabbed my head. Before either of us could say anything else, black waves flowed over my field of vision, and I faded into unconsciousness.

❖

"Are you okay?" Sloane paused to look at me before making her way into our classroom.

I hadn't gained consciousness this morning until hours later, when my alarm went off. When I went to turn it off, I saw it had been ringing for almost fifteen minutes. The stabbing sensation was gone, but what was left was throbbing pain that made me acutely aware of every beat of my pulse. I gazed around my room, looking for Clara in every corner. When I finally got out of bed, I'd kept my comforter wrapped around my shoulders. I knew it gave me no real protection but needed that false sense of security to help get me moving. The terror had grown and deepened as every drop of blood, every muscle, every bone in my body felt tense and strained with the weight of Mrs. Braverman's visit and the belief that I would never feel safe again.

I had rummaged through my drawers and pulled out the first articles of clothing my hands landed on, which turned out to be a pale blue tank top and orange shorts. I dressed without showering, and when I brushed my teeth, I started at my reflection. Bluish, bruise-like half moons sat under my eyes, and I'd never been so pale.

"Rough night," I said.

"We can cancel our study date if you're not up for it."

"No. Let's study." I'd decided I needed to tell someone what was happening with Mrs. Braverman, and for whatever reason, she was adamant I not tell my father. That meant I couldn't tell Nick either because word would make its way back to Dad. "Can we still go to your house?"

"Sure. You're sure you're feeling up to it?"

"I'm sure."

"Good morning." Nick handed sheets of paper to us on his way to his desk. "Happy Friday. You good, Aria?"

"Headache."

"Sometimes the residuals of a phantom frost take a while to shake," he said.

"I think that's what it is." I didn't feel great about lying to him, but I didn't have it in me to give it a lot of thought at the moment.

"Well, we will be taking it easy today," he said. "I made some notes on the things we saw and discussed yesterday. Let's talk about the tour; you two can ask me any questions, and then I'll let you go home, and you won't have to think about ghosts again for a couple days."

"Sounds good." I didn't look at the notes he'd given us; I couldn't bear to try to make sense of the letters.

"What questions do you have?" He took his place on the edge of his desk. I hadn't actually seen him sit in his chair yet.

"Can we talk about the court proceedings?" Sloane asked.

"Sure. What do you want to know?"

"The man whose hearing we saw had been charged with emotional embezzlement. What is that, and why was he being punished for it?"

Nick walked to the blackboard. "There are two types of

crimes we manage in our court system. The first kind is earthly, and those are the crimes for which human courts do have punishments. When those kinds of issues are adjudicated at AfterCorps, it means that the prior either didn't get caught in life or that they did, but the punishment didn't suit the crime. This happens quite often with rapists, for example, who tend to have very light sentences compared to the damage they cause.

"The second kind of crime is an unearthly one. Those are the crimes for which people aren't prosecuted here in the United States but are severe enough that they keep priors from moving on. Emotional embezzlement is a perfect example of this."

Under the heading "Unearthly Crimes," Nick wrote "Emotional Embezzlement."

"Jack Dugan had a string of four relationships in which he was emotionally abusive to his partners. He made them feel terrible about themselves, gave them feelings of worthlessness, and then leveraged their pain into power over them, always making them question themselves, question what he was doing to them. The common term regs use for it is 'gaslighting,' and it's a relatively recent topic of mainstream discussion. It's been a crime punishable by the AfterCorps court system since our organization was established."

"Who established the court system?" I asked.

"Your great-great-grandfather. Myron Jasper revolutionized interpretership in so many ways—the most significant, in my opinion, is that he modeled what we do after an earthly system of checks and balances that was already in place. It's given interpreters a foundation to build our skills on, with guidelines that make sense to us. Before Myron, there were no clear-cut procedures, and interpreters were left to figure things out based on whatever information had been passed down to them. He spent his life researching different rituals and practices performed by hundreds of interpreters and streamlined them into something solid and practical."

"And priors are punished with dominion service, which I'm guessing is like community service?" Sloane asked.

"Sort of. It's imperative that we create a punishment that fits the crime. It's the only way to achieve the kind of balance that allows priors to start out in the afterworld with a clean slate."

"What was Jack Dugan's punishment?" I asked.

"He had to shadow a reg who was being emotionally abused and gaslit. He existed with a woman who was going through an excruciating relationship and went through every emotion along with her, never leaving her side throughout dominion service and taking on a portion of the emotional ramifications. It's a punishment to have to go through that, and it is a service, as well. The reg he shadowed never knew he was there, of course, but she didn't have to bear the entire brunt of the abuse."

I didn't know what to say, and I guessed Sloane didn't either because she remained silent. On one hand, it seemed awesome that there were punishments for the kinds of crimes for which nobody seemed to suffer when they were alive. On the other, I couldn't help but think of Clara, who seemed an example of a judicial system that was failing. My head throbbed more intensely when I considered her and my own messy situation for which I had no answers.

"Other questions?" Nick asked.

"How does the chief of transfers lose their eyesight?" I asked. "And who made that rule?"

"Only your father and the COT know that. What else?"

Frustration flared in me. I'd had to fight for every shred of information about interpreting and AfterCorps, and most of what I learned only opened up dozens more questions. Nick was more forthright than my father, but even he seemed guarded about what and how much to share. How were Sloane and I supposed to prepare ourselves for whatever lay ahead when the whole system was set up as a game for which the rules constantly changed?

"Is there anything that will help Aria get over her phantom frost headache?" Sloane asked, and my heart filled with gratitude.

"Heat helps a little. A hot shower does wonders, or if that's not available, a warm washcloth."

The one day I skipped a shower.

❖

"I'll drive," Sloane said. "I can bring you back for your car when we're done."

I didn't feel well enough to argue, so I let her guide me to her car and dropped into the passenger seat when she opened the door. Moments after she started driving, I fell asleep. I woke to her resting her hand on my wrist where Clara Braverman had grasped it, and I jumped.

"Sorry," she said. "I didn't mean to scare you. We're home."

I looked around groggily, got out of the car, and followed her inside.

"Sit here." She pointed to the couch. "You can lie down if you want. I'll be right back."

I didn't want to lie on Sloane's couch, and I didn't want to be a mess in front of her, but it couldn't be helped. I stretched out on the lumpy couch and closed my eyes. I didn't think I'd fall asleep again, but I woke to a damp warmth on my head. Sloane was kneeling on the floor beside me, holding a washcloth to my face. I felt the edges of my headache begin to smooth out and soften.

"Thank you," I said.

"No thanks needed. Just rest for a while. I'll keep the warm washcloths coming."

"You don't have to do that." I began to sit up.

She cupped my chin with her free hand. "Rest. Please."

The "please" did me in, and I set my head back down. I slept for several hours, waking only when Sloane placed a newly warmed washcloth on my head. Finally, I opened my eyes. The pain had mostly subsided, and I was able to take a look around. Sloane sat on the floor a few feet away, reading our textbook. She looked up when she saw me and came over.

"How are you feeling, champ?" she asked.

"Better, thanks to you."

She smiled and took my hand to help me sit up. My mouth was very dry. "Could I have some water?" I asked.

"Sure." She was gone only moments before returning with a bottle of cold water. I drank the entire thing within minutes. I was starting to feel more human again.

"Hopefully, you'll be good as new before you know it," she said. Her gray eyes darkened. "Aria?"

"Yeah?"

"What's going on with you? Is this really a phantom frost headache from yesterday? You didn't seem this bad on the tour, and you were fine when you sang. Better than fine."

"You're right." I got down on the floor and sat facing her, our knees touching. I felt nervous all of a sudden. What if she didn't believe me or thought I was crazy? I looked into her eyes, filled with questions and concern, and knew that now was the time. "I have to tell you something. I think you're the only person I can tell, but you have to keep it a secret."

"Okay."

"Promise?" I extended my pinkie finger. She linked her pinkie with mine, then pulled my hand to her mouth and kissed it.

"I promise." Her eyes were almost silver, and it was several seconds before I realized I had a dopey smile on my face. A potent twinge of happiness cut through all my fear and nervousness, and I felt surer of my decision to open up to her.

"Okay." I took a deep breath. "A prior has been…visiting me."

"What do you mean?"

"The ghost Nick was talking about the other day, the one I saw for the first time at the funeral home, she's come to me twice at my house. That's the reason I had such a bad headache all day. She grabbed my wrist this morning, and it caused that phantom frost, which was, incidentally, the absolute worst pain I've ever felt in my life."

"I'm confused. Why didn't you let your dad handle it?"

"He wasn't around. The first time I was in the upstairs hallway, and he was all the way down in the kitchen. This morning, he would've already left for work."

"But...but that can't be." She shook her head.

"I guess Nick was wrong about not being able to communicate with priors without a guardian until after training. I mean, it's not like ghosts can tell when you've had training or not..." I trailed off because she was still shaking her head.

"You haven't been released."

"Released?"

"Yeah, it's a whole thing. Your guardian and a few elder interpreters perform a ceremony releasing you to be able to communicate with priors without the ward of protection every child of an interpreter gets at birth. It's the equivalent of learning to walk. While you're learning, your parents hold your hands or make sure you have something solid to hang on to. When you're ready, they let go, and only then can you walk on your own, right?"

"Right."

"That's what happens when you're released."

"I'm not sure I totally understand that," I said.

She shrugged. "Nobody does until it happens. What I just told you is the explanation my mom gave me when I started asking about it a few years ago."

"Hmm. It doesn't make sense, then. I know what I saw." If what she said was true, and I had no reason to doubt it, something was very, very wrong, more than I'd even realized. I wondered if I would ever know what it was like to not be always afraid again. I wondered how many more terrifying blows I could take.

She held my hand. "I believe you and what you saw. I just

don't understand how it can be happening. I wonder why she's coming to you?"

I filled her in on everything Mrs. Braverman had said, giving her every detail I could remember and probably more than she wanted to hear. If she was going to help me, I wanted her to have the complete picture.

"Sounds a little scary," she said when I was done.

"It's been very scary," I said, and before I could stop myself, I blurted, "I started sleeping with a night-light again."

"I don't blame you. After hearing your story, I might buy myself one."

"You never had a night-light?"

"Nope. The dark never bothered me."

"Tough stuff, huh?" I smiled. I wished I had some of her cool confidence.

"Nah. Darkness is where the real is. Anything can seem nice in the daylight."

"That's true." I looked at her hand on mine, and she looped our fingers together so they were interlaced. I turned my gaze to find her staring, and seconds later, she leaned in and kissed me.

Her lips were soft as they brushed mine, and I tasted a little of the mango pineapple ChapStick she used. The last of the chill in my head slipped away as the warmth of her mouth brought heat to the surface. I put my hand on her cheek and deepened our kiss, enjoying the feel of her tongue against mine. It lasted less than a minute, but I had to gasp for air when we pulled our mouths apart, my heart was pounding so hard.

It had been a long time since I'd been kissed, and I'd never been kissed like that. I really liked this girl. She was the only good to come from all the terrible I'd endured recently, and I couldn't imagine how I would have gotten through it without her.

"What time is it?" I asked.

She dug in her pocket for her phone. "Almost four o'clock."

I'd slept longer than I planned. "I should go soon."

"I drove, remember? I need to take you back to your car."

"Well, now I remember," I said, and she laughed. I stood and held my hands down to help her. She kissed me on the forehead after she took my hand and stood.

"So you're really not going to tell your dad about the prior?" she asked once we were in the car.

"Mrs. Braverman is so adamant that I don't. I don't think I can."

"Why would she think your dad is a bad man?" she asked, frowning. "He's a great man."

"I think so too. I guess everyone is the bad guy to somebody."

"I think you should tell him."

"Why?"

"Look what happened to you this morning," she said. "And how long it took you to recover. It could be dangerous."

"Sloane, we're beginning a career working with ghosts. Our entire lives from this point could be dangerous if this is what happens when they get angry. I'm sure not all priors are going to be happy about their situations."

She paused to concentrate on changing lanes. "I just don't want you to get hurt."

"I know. I don't think Mrs. Braverman was trying to hurt me. Neither of us knew what to expect."

"Thank you for telling me what's going on. I want to help."

"I think you can," I said. "Will you ask your mom about this stuff? My dad will be suspicious. But you've been having in-depth discussions about being an interpreter with your mom forever, and it won't be out of the ordinary if you ask her under what circumstances someone might start seeing ghosts before the release, right?" I was nervous about asking her to talk to her mom under false pretenses, but I was at a loss as to what else to try. I'd been pulled into this web of lies against my will, but now that I was here, it seemed like the only thing to do was play the game the way everyone else was playing.

We pulled into the parking lot, and she put her car in park

beside mine. "I can probably come up with a way to slide it under the radar in a convo."

"Great," I said, a sigh of relief coming out behind the word. "I really appreciate it. Thank you for the ride too."

"You're welcome. You're good to drive now, right?"

"Yeah, I feel good." I didn't tell her that her kiss had healed me, even though that was how I felt.

"Good. Text me when you get home so I know you made it."

I was touched at how much she had cared for me today, and even now she was concerned about me getting home. "I will," I leaned over and gave her a quick kiss. "I'll talk to you soon."

CHAPTER EIGHTEEN

Friday afternoon, every sound our old house had made caused me to startle, and I found myself constantly glancing around to see if Mrs. Braverman was there. My parents finally noticed.

"Is everything all right, Aria?" Mom asked at dinner after I'd returned from Sloane's house. "You seem jumpy."

"Yeah. Just getting over a headache. I'll probably go to bed early tonight." I had a momentary shock at how easy it was becoming to lie but brushed it off as best I could. My parents had lied to me my whole life, and I suspected, continued to do so. If this was what I had to do to protect myself, I'd do it.

I went to bed early, and Saturday morning I woke with a jerk, sitting up and looking around in the gentle glow of my night-light. It wasn't even six o'clock, hours before I'd normally wake up on a Saturday. I grabbed my cell phone and sent a text to Macy. We'd been planning to hang out in the afternoon, so I invited her over for our first slumber party since my birthday. When she texted back at seven to say she'd love to sleep over, I breathed deeply and realized how shallow my breaths had been. It was crazy to think about all the ways my life had changed since a little over a month ago, not the least of which was how relieved I was to not be sleeping alone that night.

I lay down and fell back to sleep. I didn't wake up again until eleven, and it was time to get up and take a shower.

As I got ready to meet Macy, I thought about my conversation with Sloane the previous day, and how she said I hadn't been released to interact with priors on my own. What could it mean that I hadn't been released, yet Mrs. Braverman could creep up on me without warning and without a protective guardian around? I realized in that moment that I was going to have to shelve my plan to run away to Los Angeles. If I got out there and was confronted by a prior, I'd have nobody to turn to. I waited for disappointment and anguish to settle in as my plans changed once again, but those feelings didn't come. Finally, I was making my own decisions based on what I'd learned so far. It felt like the beginning of getting solid ground under my feet again.

I met Macy at the park where we used to play. Sometimes, we would still swing side by side just like in elementary school when our moms sat on the benches. Today, we walked on the trail that circled the park, then went back through a wooded area next to a pond. We sat at a picnic table and looked into the water.

After a few minutes of comfortable silence, Macy asked, "Do you want to talk about it?"

"Talk about what?"

"Whatever has you looking like…" She clamped her mouth shut.

"Like?"

"I was going to say 'like you've seen a ghost,' but I realized that saying isn't even a joke anymore."

"No, it's definitely not." I bent down, picked up a smooth stone, and ran it between my thumb and index finger. I flicked my wrist and flung it into the pond, watching it skip three times before it disappeared beneath the ripples.

"Have you seen a lot of them?" Macy asked. "Ghosts, I mean."

"I've seen a few. We took a tour of AfterCorps and saw a lot of them. But only one has been bothering me."

My parents hadn't told me not to discuss AfterCorps or being an interpreter with Macy, but it seemed like an unspoken rule. She was a reg, and regs led very different lives. She had been there the night I'd seen my first prior, so I assumed my parents knew I'd told her at least a little bit about it. I was sure they'd frown on me divulging a lot of details, though.

More than that, I'd been hesitant to talk to Macy too much about what had been happening because I didn't know how she could possibly relate. As much as I'd give anything to be a reg whose biggest concern was trying to find a job and hanging around by the pool, that wasn't who I was anymore. Was it even fair to trouble her with issues that were completely outside the realm of what was normal for her, stuff she should never even have to think about as long as she was alive?

I looked into her wide eyes with their furrowed brows, the way they always looked when she was concerned, and I realized how much I'd been missing her and how hard it had been to navigate all of this without my best friend. And then I was telling her everything: AfterCorps and its hierarchy, the court system with its crimes and punishments I didn't understand, the blind man who chose to lose his vision so he could lead priors to their last destination, and how scared I was after receiving these visits from Mrs. Braverman.

"You don't have to sleep over if you don't want to," I said after I told her that last part. "If it's too scary, you don't have to spend the night."

Macy linked her arm through mine. "Of course I'm going to stay the night. If that ghost comes back, I want to be there with you."

"Thank you." If our situations were reversed, I didn't know if I would have been so brave. Not that I would've let Macy go through something like that alone, but it wouldn't have been as easy as she was making it seem.

"You know what I think?" Macy asked.

"What?"

"I think we need to go stock up on some serious snacks. Popcorn is in order, but we're gonna need more than that. I'm talking about calling in the heavy hitters: Milk Duds, hot wings, Tahitian Treat, Doritos. Real get-down-to-business foods."

"Let's hit the store. Might wanna add Tums to our list."

Macy frowned. "What, are we amateurs now?"

❖

Several hours later, we settled into the basement with plates, bowls, and bags of food between us.

"We're never going to eat all this," I said.

"The night is young." Macy dipped a hot wing into some bleu cheese dressing and took a bite. "Don't underestimate us."

I pushed play on the movie we'd chosen—*Slumber Party Massacre*—and started laughing almost immediately at the early '80s hair and fashion.

"Look at those short shorts." Macy cackled. "And with the socks pulled all the way up too. Who thought that could possibly look good?"

"Oh, you'd be surprised, dear. I've seen more than my fair share of ridiculous fashions in my day, and I've always found that the worst culprits think they look the best."

I froze with my hand halfway to the bag of Milk Duds and sat staring at Clara Braverman.

"What?" Macy asked. "Aria, what is it?"

"She's here," I whispered.

"The ghost?"

Clara shook her head. "I don't like that."

"What, being called a ghost?"

"Yes. I'm a person. A deceased person but a person nonetheless."

"What's happening?" Macy asked.

"She doesn't like being called a ghost. It's Mrs. Braverman. You can probably just call her that."

Clara nodded. "That'll be fine."

"What can I do for you, Clara?" My tone matched the coolness I felt in my bones at her presence.

"I came to apologize. I had no idea that my touching you would affect you so severely. I didn't mean to hurt you."

"Thank you," I said. "It did hurt a lot. I had a headache that felt like my brain was trying to eat itself, and it took me all day to feel better. Please make sure not to touch me from now on."

"I will. I truly am sorry."

"I accept your apology."

Macy had set down her hot wing but still had sauce all over her hands and face, and she was staring at the corner where Clara stood. Clara noticed it too and gave a little wave. She laughed when Macy continued to stare with no indication that she could see.

"Your friend is probably lucky she can't see me," Clara said.

"I wish I couldn't," I muttered.

"I understand that. But you can, and I need your help, desperately."

I sighed. "Yes, you've told me, but I don't know the first thing about trying to help you, especially since you don't want me to ask my dad, and I'm assuming that means Nick is out too. You won't let me go to the people who actually know what to do."

"Because they are the reason I'm still here."

"And you're sure that reason isn't a good one?"

A cloud of tears formed in Clara's eyes, and again I started to wonder about ghosts and their bodily functions. How could a ghost even make tears if she didn't have a body?

"I loved Sol," she said, and her voice shook. "He was my husband, and I loved him. I didn't kill him, nobody did."

"Okay," I said. "But what can I do?"

"You must find a way to help me transfer," she said. "Get me into the transfer room. I can figure out how to get to my destination from there."

"I can't do that."

"Please, Aria." Her presence began to flicker like a lightbulb whose life was at an end. "Please, you must." And then she was gone.

❖

"You know," Macy said, somehow ready to dive into the Doritos after I filled her in, "it shouldn't be too hard to find out how her husband died. I'm sure there's an obituary, and if it doesn't say in there, there's sure to be a death certificate. Didn't you tell me she had an autopsy done on him?"

"Yeah." I grabbed one of the hot wings and bit into it. It had gotten cold, but it was still pretty good.

"So there's paperwork that would verify his cause of death," Macy said.

"True. But wouldn't an autopsy be done in a hospital? Those records wouldn't be public, would they?"

"No, I guess not. Let's start with Google and see if we can find the obit." She brushed her hands on a paper towel and grabbed her phone, typing and scrolling while I ate another wing and washed it down with some Tahitian Treat. Opening up to Sloane and Macy had been the right thing to do. I felt so much better now that I wasn't trying to process and deal with all of this by myself.

"There," she said. "Found it." She scooted close to me so we could read it together.

"No cause of death listed. But it does ask that donations be made to the American Heart Association."

Macy stared across the room and munched on some popcorn. "So the seed about it being a heart issue was definitely planted."

"Right, but we don't know for sure. I know my dad and Nick write a lot of obituaries, but they get all the information from the families."

"Do you think your dad found out something when he was

helping Mrs. Braverman plan her husband's funeral and just held on to it until she died?"

"No way. If he found out something, he would've gone to the police."

"Are you sure?" Her brown eyes had darkened so that I couldn't distinguish between the pupils and irises.

"Why wouldn't he?"

"Well," she said slowly, "if he knew he could essentially be judge and jury after Mrs. Braverman passed, your dad might have decided to bide his time and wait until a proper punishment could be given."

"My dad's not like that," I said, but even as the words came out, I realized they might not be true. I'd found out a lot of new information about my dad in the last several weeks. He'd been living a double life, and I never had a clue. It hit me that I truly didn't know what he was capable of. I hadn't considered that Clara could be right about him. My head swam with the awful possibilities.

Macy fidgeted with some Milk Duds before popping them into her mouth. "Do you wanna go back to watching our movie?"

"Sure." I leaned back and tried to focus on the terrible slasher instead of the endless thoughts running through my mind.

❖

We'd watched *Slumber Party Massacre* parts one and two and had eaten all the hot wings, popcorn, Milk Duds, and most of the Doritos when I got a text. It was almost midnight, and usually the only person who would message me that late was right next to me.

"Who's that?" Macy asked.

"It's Sloane." Just saying her name brought heat to my cheeks.

"*Oh*," Macy drawled. "What does Cutie McHot Lips have to say?"

"She asked her mom about seeing priors before the release ceremony, and she needs to talk to me right away."

"Sounds serious. We should invite her over."

"Now?"

"She said right away, didn't she? And as your best friend, I need to meet the girl you've had the biggest crush on since Kristen Stewart."

"I didn't crush on Kristen Stewart. I crushed on Kristen Stewart playing Joan Jett. Big difference."

"Whatever. Are you gonna text her back, or what?"

"Fine." I texted Sloane and told her I was hanging out with Macy, and that if it was that important, she could come over. "She's gonna say no."

"Why would she say no?"

"Why would she say yes?" I asked, and then my phone went off again. "She said yes."

Macy jumped up and looked like the Tasmanian Devil if Taz had been super into cleaning. "I'll get this room tidied up. You go get ready."

"Get ready?"

She rolled her eyes. "Aria, get it together. Go change clothes, brush your hair. Maybe wash up a little so you don't smell like Doritos and hot wings when your lady love gets here."

I went upstairs and took a five-minute shower and changed. I even brushed my teeth and used mouthwash and then went down to the living room to wait with Macy.

I'd told Sloane to text when she got there so Macy and I could sneak her in and shuffle her to the basement without my parents knowing there was a cute girl visiting me in the middle of the night.

Here, Sloane's text buzzed on my phone.

I crept to the door and opened it, and Sloane tiptoed inside.

I took her hand, grateful for the darkness so she couldn't see me blush, and led her down to the basement with Macy following. I made the introductions and was pleased when Sloane hugged Macy.

"I've heard a lot about you," Sloane said.

"Oh, same here. You have no idea."

"Oh, really?" Sloane arched an eyebrow at me. "You've been talking about me?"

"Only in regard to your terrible taste in music," I said, but my blush probably told the truth. I'd never talked about a crush or someone I'd dated as much as I talked about Sloane. I'd never like anyone as much either.

"Hey, all press is good press." She sat on the love seat with me, and Macy sat in the recliner facing us.

"Mrs. Braverman paid us a visit tonight," I said and filled Sloane in on what had happened.

"We checked out the obituary." Macy pulled out her phone and let Sloane take a look.

"American Heart Association," she murmured. "Interesting."

"I wish we could take a look at the death certificate," I said.

"Well," Sloane began slowly, "no, never mind."

"What?" Macy asked and scooted to the edge of her seat.

"There would be a copy at the funeral home. I'm almost positive. When my grandma died, the coroner issued the certificate, but when we needed a copy, we had to go through the funeral home to get it."

"It's probably a digital file," Macy said. "That's my guess, anyway. Does your dad bring a laptop home?"

"No. If we go on vacation or he takes time off for the holidays, he'll bring it with him, but the rest of the time, he leaves it at work."

"Well, I guess we'll have to sneak into the office soon," Sloane said. I thought she was joking, but her expression was serious.

"Really?" I asked.

"You asked me to help with this, right? And the best way to figure out why Mrs. Braverman is still here and how to get her moved on is to get our questions answered."

"That's true." I'd made my peace with lying, as it seemed to be essential to my survival. But breaking and entering? That was next level, and even though I couldn't see a way around it if we were going to get the answers we needed, I didn't feel great about it.

"Aw, look at you two," Macy said. "The couple who breaks into funeral homes together stays together."

"Shut up," I told her, but Sloane laughed and took my hand.

"Hopefully that's true," she said. Crooked smile. Blush. I hoped it didn't freak Sloane out to hear someone refer to us as a couple. "Listen, before we get too sidetracked, I need to tell you what my mom said."

"Okay. Is it bad?"

"Not bad. Just confusing. I feel like the more answers we get, the more questions we have."

I was relieved to hear her verbalize what I'd been feeling since we started training. "What do you mean?"

"She told me that the only time she knew of people who could communicate with priors before they were released was when they inherited interpretation from both parents, but only one parent made the ward of protection at birth. The ward is designed to protect the DNA from the parent who places the ward, but it doesn't protect from dual parentage."

"Well, there has to be another reason that she doesn't know about," I said. "My mom isn't an interpreter."

"You're sure about that?" Macy asked.

"I'm pretty sure, yeah."

"I mean, you just found out about your dad," Macy said. "This whole world exists that you never even knew about. Isn't it possible that your mom could be an interpreter?"

Another brick had been added to the weight I carried, and I felt myself crumble underneath it all. It seemed not only impossible but also unbearable to consider that my mom wasn't who I believed her to be and that the lie my parents had told might be even bigger than I thought.

I turned to Sloane. "You tell us. You're the one who was brought up as an interpreter, and you know all about my dad and his history in AfterCorps. You know more about my heritage than anyone. Have you ever heard about my mother being an interpreter?"

"As far as I know, your mom is a reg. She's aware of AfterCorps, of course. She essentially runs the surface business for your dad since his responsibilities as a special are a full-time job and then some."

"Right. So, it has to be something else. Did your mom have anything else to say about it?"

"That was all she knew."

"That was the emergency you had to come over in the middle of the night to tell us about?" Macy smirked.

"Hey, I didn't tell you I needed to come over. But I wasn't going to turn down the invitation."

"You know what?" Macy asked, and she stood. "We need more snacks."

"*More* snacks?" My stomach turned over a little at the thought of more junk food after all we'd consumed already.

"I'm being a good hostess. Sloane hasn't eaten anything. Besides, I need more popcorn if we're going to watch another movie. Sloane, can you stay and watch one with us?"

"Sure. And popcorn sounds great."

"Awesome," Macy said, and she shuffled upstairs.

Sloane brushed her fingers across my forehead. "How's the nog?"

"Better. Thanks to you." A warmth spread across my head where her fingers traced my skin, and my pulse quickened.

"I'm glad," she whispered, and our faces were so close. She kissed my forehead, her lips skimming my hairline, then my eyelids, and then her mouth was on mine. It wasn't a deep kiss like we'd had the day before, but a gentle one. Our lips parted, and she rested her hand on my shoulder. She pulled back and looked into my eyes. "I'm going to protect you."

"Protect me from what?" I was simultaneously happy and concerned. I loved that she wanted to protect me, but I knew that, in the event that Clara did try to hurt me, there would be very little Sloane could do. She couldn't even interact with a prior without her guardian present.

Her gray eyes darkened as if a cloud passed across them. "It's not right that your father kept you in the dark about AfterCorps all these years. It's good work, important work, but there are aspects of it that are more dangerous than you know. I don't even know the extent of the danger, but at least I've been prepared for the fact that what I'll be doing could get me hurt, and I know the basics of what's expected. You're coming to this completely unprepared."

"And you think that's going to put me in danger?"

"It already has. Look what's been happening to you."

"But that's not my dad's fault."

"Isn't it?" She touched my head again.

"Snacks!" Macy appeared at the bottom of the stairs with a bowl of popcorn and a second bag of Milk Duds I hadn't even seen her buy.

I dragged a third bean bag chair out from the corner and sat between Sloane and Macy. We watched *Leprechaun 4*, the one where they go to space. With a lot of effort, I was able to focus on the terrible movie and the feel of Sloane's hand on my leg. At the end, Sloane said she needed to be getting home, and I told her I'd walk her out.

We stood next to her car together, and she leaned in for a hug. We held each other for a couple minutes before she pulled back, touched my chin, and kissed me. I realized every time we kissed, it made me hungry for more. I wanted to kiss her when it wasn't time for one of us to leave; I wanted long, lingering kisses, deep and hard and soft and slow. I wanted all of her kisses, and that wasn't all I wanted.

"Aria," she breathed.

"Yeah?" I tried to keep my own breath even.

"After that movie you just made me watch, I don't ever want to hear about my taste in music again."

I grinned. "No promises."

CHAPTER NINETEEN

On Monday, Nick announced we'd be getting our first field agent apprentice assignments by the end of the week.

"I thought we were supposed to intern with the clerks first," Sloane said.

"Normally, you'd be right," he said. "But since you two are a little late to the party, we are doing some accelerated plans. You'll go over and shadow the clerks a bit this week, probably Wednesday and Thursday, see what they do and what the day-to-day is for them. It won't be a formal apprenticeship like you would have had if you'd quickened at eighteen or twenty. The goal is to get you guys up to speed so you'll be ready to become full interpreters by twenty-five. That means we have a lot to cover in a short amount of time, so we need to condense some things."

"Does that mean we won't be learning as much?" A few days ago, I wouldn't have minded that our training was going to be shorter than expected, and it surprised me to realize I cared about learning everything I could. Somehow, I'd begun to want to know all the ins and outs of being an interpreter.

"Not at all. You're still getting all the knowledge you need; we've just sped up the pace."

I wasn't completely sold. If most interpreters started their training by the time they were twenty, we were a full two years behind. How could they really cram five years of training into three years and say it was just as good?

Nick must have guessed my thought process. "Listen, when trainees come in here at eighteen or twenty, a lot of what we do is develop the maturity to handle what is happening. We can skip most of that with you guys because not only are you twenty-two, you're both mature in general. We also only train two or three days a week when the quickening happens that early, as opposed to bringing you in for five days."

"What happens when I start my field agent assignment, as far as my surface job?" I asked. "It's going to be tough scheduling singing for funerals around me being out in the field, right?"

"Your parents have decided that for your portion of assignment training, you'll only be performing the aspects that get completed here at AfterCorps," Nick said. "You won't be going into the field."

"Really?" I asked. "Why?"

He shook his head. "Your parents are still doing a bang-up job of telling you what's going on with your own life, I see." Those deep grooves appeared again on his forehead, and he rubbed his temples. "It was a condition your mother set."

"But why?" I couldn't understand my parents. They wanted me to give up everything to go to ghost training, and now that I was here, they were putting caveats on what I could do and how much I could learn. It made no sense.

"Talk to them," he said, and it felt as if his voice stabbed me. He softened a bit. "I'll speak to your father again on your behalf. He needs to do a much better job of keeping you informed. He acts as if none of this even affects you."

"I agree," Sloane said.

"Yeah," I said. "Me too."

Fresh anger swelled in me. I'd been so angry that I wasn't going to live the life I'd planned that I hadn't spent enough time examining why this life had been so hidden. My parents had known there was more than a fifty percent chance I'd be an interpreter, yet they'd let me build my dreams around my musical aspirations. They knew being an interpreter was dangerous and had left me unprepared and unprotected. They hadn't been able to control whether I inherited the interpreter gene, but they had complete control over how they communicated with me since my quickening, and they were doing it very badly.

"Nick," I said. "Would you be willing to sit and talk to my parents with me? I'm getting all my information through you, and I know you're not comfortable telling me what is obviously stuff I should be hearing from them. Maybe if we talk to them together, they'll be more willing to give up the goods."

"You want to strong-arm them into telling you everything?" he asked, a small smile on his face.

"If that's what it takes, yeah."

"Let me think about it. You might be on to something."

Now that I was invested in learning what it would take to be an interpreter, I didn't want the half-assed version of training, nor was I willing to continue to accept my parents robbing me of knowledge that would inform my decisions and keep me from harm. I hoped Nick would agree to help me, but I was going to get some answers, with or without him.

❖

"Hey," Sloane said after class, "when is the next funeral you're singing at?"

"Wednesday afternoon. Why?"

"I was thinking, maybe that would be a good time for me to poke around in the office and see what I can find about Mrs. Braverman."

"By yourself?"

"Yeah, think about it." She spoke faster when she got excited. "Everyone is busy during the funerals; they don't have time to hang out in the office. Your mom, the one who usually goes in and out, will be accompanying you on the piano, right? So she won't be in there. It's perfect."

"Snooping around the office when the funeral home is packed isn't exactly perfect."

"Okay, not perfect. But it's a decent plan."

"It's an okay plan."

"Fine, fine." She laughed. "If we come up with a better plan before Wednesday, we'll do that. If we don't, will you at least think about this one?"

"I'll think about it."

❖

But on Wednesday, we hadn't come up with a better plan. I'd been racking my brain looking for opportunities to sneak, and short of breaking in after hours, I couldn't think of an idea better than Sloane's.

"Aria?"

"Huh?" I broke from my deep thoughts to see Sandy Dennison, Sloane's mom, staring at me.

"I was telling you how we process the field agent assignment paperwork after we get the information to the priors," she said.

I'd been sitting at Sandy's station all morning, learning how to establish the start of prior-field agent relationships and the importance of good customer service and thorough explanations, as well as detail oriented processing procedures.

When Nick told me that I'd be shadowing Sandy, I felt as if it was the perfect opportunity to score some brownie points and make an awesome impression with my crush's—or possibly my girlfriend's—mom.

Instead, I'd been distracted, my mind busy trying to think of a better solution to the Mrs. Braverman problem than having

Sloane snoop around when there would be close to a hundred people milling about in the building.

"Are you okay, love?" Sandy's eyes were brown, not gray, but her eyebrows furrowed the same way Sloane's did when she was concerned. "Are you feeling all right?"

"Yes. I'm sorry. I...I have to sing at a funeral this afternoon. I guess I'm already thinking about that. I don't think I'll have time to do a run-through like I normally do."

She smiled. "I can let you go a little early if that will help."

"It might. Thank you."

"No problem. Here, take these papers over to Janet at the other end of the counter, will you?"

"Sure." I took the stack of forms.

Sloane was shadowing Janet, and if I could get her away for a moment, maybe I could make a last-ditch effort to talk her out of sneaking into the office.

"Sandy asked me to give you these," I told Janet.

"Thank you, dear."

"Hey, I'll walk you back over there," Sloane said. "I need to ask my mom something, if that's okay with you, Janet?"

"Of course, that's fine."

"Are you still planning on going through with this madness?" I whispered as we took baby steps back to her mother's station.

"Have you come up with anything else?" she asked.

"You know I haven't." I scowled.

"Look, I'm not going to do this if you're dead set against it. I think it's our best shot right now, but if you think it's that bad an idea, I'll scrap it, and we can figure something out later."

"I don't know. Your mom is letting me leave early to go practice. Do you think you can cut out a little early too? Meet me upstairs?"

"I'll see what I can do."

"Sloane," Sandy said when she saw us. "How's Janet treating you?"

"She's sweet. No complaints."

"Good. Maybe we can talk you into being a clerk after all?"

"I wouldn't go that far." She wrapped her mom in a tight hug when Sandy's face fell. "But anything's possible."

❖

Mom and I ran through "How Great Thou Art" a couple times before she went to take her place at the piano in the main parlor.

"Are you coming?" she asked.

"Yeah, I'm going to run to the restroom, and then I'll be there."

"Don't take too long; it's less than ten minutes before the funeral."

I stepped out into the hall and waited for Sloane. The minutes slipped by, and two minutes before the funeral started, I was getting ready to give up when I heard Sloane whisper my name from down the hallway.

"What took you so long?" I whispered. "I have to go in now."

"Sorry. Janet kept giving me more paperwork to file. Are you ready? Is this office empty?"

"I think so."

"You're sure you're okay with me doing this?"

I'd thought I'd have a couple minutes to talk things out a final time, but instead, I had about ten seconds to make the decision. "Go ahead. Just be careful."

"I will." She grabbed my wrist and whispered, "Break a leg, babe."

I sat next to my mother and made sure my chair was turned so that I could see the door to the office. I didn't have a plan in case Nick or my dad or one of the funeral goers decided to go in, but it made me feel better to have a good view.

The minister welcomed the mourners and began her short sermon, we sang a hymn, and the deceased's son gave a eulogy.

Finally, it was my turn to sing, and when I was finished, there would be a prayer, and the funeral would be over. I stood, and my mother played the intro. I breathed deeply and began to sing. I had just gotten to the end of the first verse when my dad passed behind the last row of people with an empty box of tissues and went toward the office. I wanted to lunge past the people in their folding chairs and put myself between the door and my father, but that wasn't an option. Instead, I kept singing as my dad opened the door and went in, closing it behind him.

I was nearly to the end of the song when he came back out with a new box of tissues and handed them to a bereaved woman. I finished the last note, my voice much steadier and stronger than I felt, and sat.

I hurried to the empty office at the end of the service and got my purse out of the coat closet. I hadn't seen Sloane leave, and she was nowhere in sight, and I was worried that something had gone very wrong. She could have exited through the back hallway, but why would she go without telling me? I texted to ask what happened. By the time my phone buzzed, I was almost to my car where she was waiting for me.

"Did my dad see you?" I asked.

"What? No. He came into the office?"

"Tissue refill. Did you find anything?"

"Nope. I looked through all the drawers, but there wasn't much of anything in terms of paperwork besides funeral arrangement agreements, and even those were over five years old. I'm guessing Jasper Funeral Home has gone completely digital. I tried the computer, but we didn't think about needing a password."

I groaned. "Dummies."

"Not dummies," she said. "I don't know about you, but I don't make a habit of hacking into business systems."

"And here I thought you were an expert." I frowned. "What now?"

"I'm not sure. We'll think of something."

❖

Dad decided that night would be a good one to cook burgers on the grill and eat on the patio. I made some potato salad and cut up some carrots and broccoli and arranged them on a tray with ranch dressing. Mom made her signature pecan pie, which she put in the oven right as we were sitting down to eat. Watching my parents fill their plates and fix their burgers and go about their business as if they hadn't been keeping me from the truth about my own life was infuriating. Now that the reality about who and what I was had surfaced, the lies should have stopped, and yet they were still going out of their way to keep me from learning all that I could about my abilities.

"So why do I have to stay behind at AfterCorps for my agent training when the protocol is for trainees to be out in the field?"

They both stopped and stared at me.

"And why do I keep having to hear important news about my life from Nick instead of from you guys?" The question I didn't ask, the one that consumed so many of my thoughts lately, was how could I ever trust either of them again?

"We want to keep your life as normal as possible," Mom said. "And we just thought that since you've had a lot less time to acclimate to being a special than most, it would be best to ease into your hands-on training."

"Yes, exactly," Dad said. "I know you're grown, Aria, but you have so much to learn about this world. And no matter how old you become, you're still our daughter, and your safety and well-being are of utmost importance to us."

"You weren't even going to discuss it with me?"

"Aria, listen to me," my mom began.

"No, you listen to me. You let me grow up with absolutely no idea that AfterCorps existed, let alone how all of these changes could happen. My entire life has changed in the last month, and you let me be completely unprepared for my future. You didn't tell me anything about who I am, who our family is, and now that I'm actually in training and trying to get a grip on all this, I'd think you'd be involved and wanting to participate. And I'd expect that you'd *want* me to jump in with training and learn as much as I can from the only people who've been willing to teach me." The words tumbled out of me as if propelled by the force of the frustration and anger that had been building toward my parents since the night I saw my first ghost.

"Dad, everyone I've met at AfterCorps has so much to say about you, about our family, my great-great-grandfather. They have expectations that I don't know the first thing about because even now, you're keeping me in the dark. You're the great leader of AfterCorps, the one everyone talks about, admires, respects." Everyone I'd come across at AfterCorps knew so much more about my family than I did, and it was crushing. Why was I such a stranger to who we really were? "You haven't shared anything about my heritage with me, and I want to know why!"

My parents were silent. They looked at each other for a long time before my dad cleared his throat. "This hasn't been easy for us, Aria. As much pride as I take in being an interpreter and in being a Jasper, it can be very, very dangerous work. We shielded you, not because we wanted you to be ill-equipped, but because we desperately wanted you to have a normal life. Your musical talents, while quite extraordinary, are not supernatural, and I—"

Mom rested her hand on his arm. "I think we hoped, rather naively as it turns out, that your phenomenal musical gifts were a sign that you were meant for this world, the reg world, instead of the AfterCorps world. It was foolish, and I'm very sorry that it caused this transition to be even more difficult for you."

"Okay," I said. It felt like the truth, but somehow, not the whole truth. "And now that you know I'm...meant for the AfterCorps world, why have you been keeping such distance with me?"

"I guess…I guess I wanted you to experience it as any other new interpreter would and not as the daughter of Nathan Jasper, great-great granddaughter of Myron Jasper."

Now he was outright lying. I was almost positive of it. What I didn't know was why. If he truly wanted me to experience training as anyone else would, he wouldn't have told Nick to keep me out of the field. Did my parents think I was stupid?

"If I have to do ghost school, I want to do the same kind of training any other new interpreter would." I paused. "Unless you're having second thoughts about whether I really need to do this?"

"We're not having second thoughts." My dad's voice was coarse.

"But what would happen if I just didn't become an interpreter? It can't be true that every single person who has interpreting abilities *has* to be one. There have to be people who possess the gift who just go out and become dentists or baristas or—"

"Singers?" Dad asked.

"Why not?"

He sighed. "Sure there are. But they all have to go through training first, at the end of which, everyone must make their own decisions about what to do. Most choose to stay with AfterCorps, but a few have walked away."

"It seems…wasteful to make someone go through years of training who doesn't have any interest in being an interpreter."

"You have to tell her," Mom said.

"Tell me what?"

"Those who decide not to utilize their gifts at interpreting can go out into the world and pursue whatever they wish, but it comes at a price. They must be cut off completely, not just from AfterCorps but from their family of interpreting origin."

"You mean I wouldn't be able to see you again?" That couldn't be.

He shook his head. "You can walk away from being an

interpreter, but you can't walk away from the fact that you inherited the gift. If you choose not to use it, you will create, for lack of a better word, a sort of static. It interferes with the ability of the interpreters in your life to communicate with priors clearly and is considered a major security issue. For my own safety, we would have to..." His voice wavered. "We'd have to cease all communication."

Now I'd have to choose between my dreams and my family? It seemed too terrible to be true. If I was going to have any kind of normal life, I'd have to do it without my father. None of this had been fair from that initial bombshell on the night of my quickening, and the injustice grew with every stone I turned over.

"I think I need to have some time to myself. I'm going upstairs." I grabbed my plate with the now cold burger and headed toward the screen door to go inside.

"I'm sorry we went over your head about going out in the field. We'll think more about it," Mom said. "You're right; we should have discussed it with you before making a decision."

"Thank you."

I went upstairs and texted Sloane to tell her what my parents said.

Are you okay? she asked.

I've been better. But hey, at least I got them to reconsider my field assignment.

We could end up out in the field together. She sent this with the wide-eyed emoji. *You might get sick of me.*

Doubt it. Kissing emoji.

Despite the devastating news, I was smiling when I set my phone aside to read the chapters from our textbook. I struggled with my ability to focus on the words in front of me as I kept thinking about the impossible choice I would have to make in a few years.

Later, I turned on my night-light and got into bed. I lay there, staring at the ceiling and thinking about how to find out how Clara's husband really died. Something Sloane said earlier kept rattling in my brain, and I couldn't figure out why it was significant:

"There wasn't much of anything in terms of paper…it looks like Jasper Funeral Home has gone digital."

I sat up and grabbed my phone.

Jasper Funeral Home may be digital, but AfterCorps isn't, I texted. *We've been pushing paper all day!*

The three little bubbles popped up to signify she was typing back to me. *And we'll be pushing it all day tomorrow too. You're a genius.*

Meet me in the parking lot at 8:30 tomorrow morning so we can figure out what we're gonna do?

See you then. Her text included another kiss emoji, and I sent one back before lying back down. After my roller coaster ride of an evening, I thought I wouldn't be able to sleep, but soon after my head was back on the pillow, I did.

CHAPTER TWENTY

We decided we would ask Sandy and Janet where records were stored and see if they needed help filing.

"My mom is always complaining about having to file things in the records room," Sloane said. "Besides, even if they say no, as long as we find out where it is, one of us can sneak in."

"I should be the one to sneak in this time."

"Whoever gets the best opportunity should do it," she said, and I rolled my eyes.

"Let's go."

As it turned out, we didn't even have to ask. Janet and Sandy told us our main job would be filing in the records room that day. "I've been saving all my paperwork for the last week to give to you two," Sandy said.

"Me too," Janet said. "This is happening at the best time."

"It sure is," I agreed.

They showed us to a locked door near Sandy's station, and she swiped a key fob on the monitor next to the handle to let us in. "If you have to go to the bathroom or anything, you'll have to get one of us to let you back in." She showed us into a room that was probably four times the size of a two-car garage, filled with nothing but rows of shelves with boxes of paperwork.

"Jeez," Sloane said. "When is AfterCorps going to move into the twenty-first century and get computerized?"

"Probably never," Sandy said. "There's too much at stake. We can't take the risk of being discovered, so we will be stuck with paper and ink indefinitely."

"Makes sense," I said. "What do you need us to do?"

She pointed to a table inside the door that had stacks of papers on it. She explained that each prior had a box for their paperwork that was housed here until a year after they transferred. She showed us where their information was kept and told us to make sure the paperwork went into the right box.

"Only half of this place has records for priors," Sloane said. "What's in the rest of it?"

"Oh, periodicals, newsletters, that kind of thing. It kind of died down these last few years, but AfterCorps newsletters used to be a big deal. We're modeled after traditional business corporations, you know, and we follow a lot of trends that white-collar businesses are prone to."

This interested me. Since I didn't have the same pool of knowledge Sloane did with regard to AfterCorps, a newsletter might help me get a feel for this place and our culture.

"Anyway, holler if you need help," Sandy said. "I'll be out at the counter."

"Thanks, Mom," Sloane said.

"Yes, thank you," I added.

Sandy slipped out, and when the heavy door closed behind her, Sloane and I made a beeline to the row that housed priors with last names starting with B.

"There." She pointed at a box several feet above our heads. "Braverman, Solomon."

I grabbed a small ladder at the end of the row and climbed up, almost losing my balance when I handed the heavy box down.

We opened it and started going through his papers. "If the death certificate is in here, it's probably at the bottom," I said, "since that would've been one of the first pieces of paperwork he had after he died."

Several minutes of carefully skimming documents and

setting them aside later, we got to the death certificate with a page stapled behind it.

"Cause of death, massive heart attack," Sloane read.

"What's the other page?"

She flipped to the document behind the death certificate. "It's the AfterCorps certification that the cause of death listed is actually the true cause of death."

"How would anyone at AfterCorps know that?"

"The data analysts capture all the pertinent information, remember? It's part of the report they make up."

"I thought we couldn't risk being digital," I said. Sloane was right that every time we got new information, it just brought up new questions.

"I don't think these screens work the same. For one thing, they aren't online, not the way we know it. For another, I've seen what the data analysts do. Did you ever see that old movie, *The Matrix*?"

"A long time ago. Don't tell me it's a black screen with green letters and numbers."

"That's exactly what it is," she said. "And data analysts are trained to read code...the code being every event in a human's life. It's a system developed over the last few decades; your father gathered a whole tech task force to make it happen."

"I didn't think this business would be so...so clinical."

She shrugged and went back to reading the AfterCorps certification. "Hey, look at this." She pointed to a section marked "Validation" at the bottom of the page. "It says that the cause of death was heart failure, the cause of which could not be contributed to either lifestyle or genetics, and therefore the root cause of death is inconclusive."

"Inconclusive?" I looked at the stacks of papers we'd set aside from Sol Braverman's box. "Do you think we can find more answers in here?"

"Maybe." She frowned and pulled her phone out. "We've been at this for over an hour. One of us should do some actual filing in case someone comes to check on us. We don't want them wondering what we've been doing all this time."

"They'd probably think it was something dirty," I said and giggled.

"That would be nice too." She threw me a crooked grin. "Do you want to file or keep looking through here?"

"I'll file for a bit, and then we can switch if you haven't found anything."

"Deal."

I went over to the table, grabbed some papers, and began filing while Sloane sifted through Mr. Braverman's documents. I stepped around her and the mess of papers surrounding her on the floor whenever I had to go past where she sat. We worked in silence, but it was nice. Lately, any silence around my house had been awkward when my parents and I were in the same room, and it was comforting to be together in companionable quiet.

I'd gotten about a third of the way through the papers when Sloane called for me. "Solomon filed paperwork with the courts before his transfer." She stood and met me at the end of the row, the paper shaking in her hands "He requested an investigation and punishment for crimes against him. He said Clara Braverman was responsible for his demise."

"It says that?"

"Word-for-word, look." She thrust the sheaf of papers at me.

"Holy shit. We need a copy of this."

She shook her head. "They'll want to know what we're doing if we go out there and start making copies. Let's just take these."

I nodded. "Okay." I watched her carefully place them inside her notebook, then in her backpack.

"I'll clean up the mess, and then I can help you with the filing," she said.

When Sandy came to check on us, we had finished about three-fourths of the filing, but she brought in another giant stack. "The other clerks found out you were doing the dirty work for

Janet and me and decided to really let you get a feel for the hustle we run."

"But we can't finish all this today," Sloane said.

"I know. Nick cleared us to have you again tomorrow, and when you're done, you'll get your field assignments for next week."

"Super," Sloane muttered, and I nudged her when I noticed how sad her mom looked.

"Anyway, thank you for your help today, girls. You're free to go; just be back here in the morning, okay? You'll go back to class with Nick for your next assignments in the afternoon. Sloane, I'll see you at home. I have to go to the flower shop; we've got some big arrangements that need to go out this evening, and I need to check they're all set. Dinner is in the Crock-Pot; it'll be ready by six. Go ahead and eat if I'm not home by then." She turned and held open the heavy door. Sloane gave her a quick peck on the cheek on the way out.

"Thanks," I said to her.

Once outside, I peered at Sloane, who was digging her keys out of her pocket.

"I think you hurt your mom's feelings," I said.

She sighed and shook her head. "I think you're right. She wants me to be a clerk so badly, and it's the absolute last job I would want. I try to tell her that while not making her feel like I don't respect the work she does, but it's not always easy."

"I'm sure it's not. Do you think she takes it personally?"

"A little bit, maybe. Mostly, I think she just worries. In her mind, being a clerk is the only safe job with AfterCorps. Or the safest job, anyway, and she's right about that."

"And you don't want to be safe?"

"I know you haven't been raised to know anything about AfterCorps, but your dad was still a funeral director. You already know that death comes when it comes, right? It's not that I'm reckless; I want to get all the training I possibly can so I can learn how to protect myself. But if there's anything AfterCorps has taught me, it's that life is too short to play it safe."

I didn't know if it was the brightness of the sun glaring down on us or the passion with which Sloane spoke, but her eyes were almost silver.

"I get that," I said.

"I'm glad." She draped her arms across my shoulders. "Hopefully, someday, my mom will get it too."

"She will," I said. "Your mom is great."

We hugged good-bye, and I headed home. I couldn't stop thinking about Sloane and her desire to work in what everyone agreed was the most dangerous sector of AfterCorps. I knew almost nothing about what that entailed, and I'd been so wrapped up in my own issues that I hadn't asked about what kind of risks were involved in the CDU. Since it had the name "demonic" in the title, it seemed pretty serious, and I resolved to talk about it with her soon. When I got home, I had a text from her waiting for me: *I just realized we haven't been on an actual date yet. Wanna fix that?*

Blood rushed to my face when I texted back, *Yes, I do.*

A few minutes after I texted her, my phone began ringing, and Sloane's crooked smile filled the screen.

"Hey," I answered.

"Hey, you. So my brother is flying in to spend the weekend at home tomorrow. We could wait until after he's gone to go on a date, but I wondered how you felt about tonight?"

My mind went to my clothes, hair, and makeup situation, and then I felt silly. Sloane had seen me for weeks in ratty T-shirts and faded shorts. Basically, any effort I put in would be an improvement on what she'd seen so far.

"I'm free tonight," I said.

"Great. Should we make it official and have me pick you up? Meet the parents and all that?"

I laughed. "You've already met my parents."

"As an interpreter trainee, yeah. But not as your girlfriend."

It took everything in me not to squeal with joy that she called herself my girlfriend. "Okay. What do you want to do?"

"It's a surprise. I'll pick you up at seven."

"But what should I wear?"

"Whatever you want. Just make sure your shoes are comfortable."

For the first time in weeks, I didn't mind that someone close to me wanted to withhold information. I used to love surprises before this recent string of unpleasant ones, and it felt good to be excited about the unknown rather than filled with dread.

CHAPTER TWENTY-ONE

After I showered, I slipped on some ripped jeans, my black Converse, and a graphic tee with a red guitar on it that said, "I love rock and roll," something I figured Sloane would appreciate.

My parents were in the living room when I went downstairs.

"Are you wearing makeup?" Mom looked as if she was trying not to smirk and failing. Normally, I only wore makeup when I was onstage, but I had lined my eyes black, run mascara through my lashes, and swiped some gloss across my lips.

"A little bit," I said.

"Well, you must be quite taken with this girl. I couldn't get you to wear makeup for any of your high school dances."

"I usually went to my dances with Macy and our other friends. They weren't dates."

"Makeup is reserved for singing and dates only," Dad said. "Now we know."

I tried to appreciate their attempts at normalcy, but it felt forced and false. It was hard to be torn between wanting to enjoy hanging out with my parents and being so suspicious of them. Before I could respond to their banter, the doorbell rang. When I answered, I lost my breath. Sloane wore a short sleeved white button-down, a red and black striped tie done loosely around her collar, and jeans ripped like mine, only several shades darker. She looked incredible.

"You're beautiful," she said.

"You are too." I heard my dad's familiar throat clearing and opened the door wider to let her in.

She crossed the room and shook my parents' hands as if she hadn't met them before.

"Good to see you again, Sloane," Dad said.

"Good to see you too."

"What are you girls up to tonight?" Mom asked.

"Yeah," I said, "what are we up to?"

"It's kind of a surprise for Aria," Sloane said. "Would it be okay if we filled you in on the details after I pull it off?"

My mom's smile widened. "Well, of course, that would be lovely. Did you hear that, honey?" She turned to my dad. "Aria gets a surprise date. Remember when you used to surprise me?"

"Many moons, my dear, many moons," Dad said.

"Well, this isn't embarrassing at all." I attempted a smile at my father, but it felt weak. I hated how hard he was trying to connect with me now after all these weeks of distance.

"Okay, okay," Mom said. "You're free to go; have a wonderful time."

We went to the car, and Sloane opened my door, bowing a little and making a sweeping motion with her arm when I got in.

"You're really not telling me where we're going?" I asked.

"Nope." Surprising me sure did bring out the adorable crookedness of her grin.

❖

Sloane parallel parked on the edge of the Short North, Columbus's art district.

"Are we going to a gallery?" I'd been guessing for the entire drive.

"No, and you just hit twenty questions, so I win."

"I don't remember making that deal. What do you win?"

"The end of the questions." She laughed. We got out of the

car and held hands as we began to walk. A few blocks later, we came to the Newport Music Hall, and Sloane held her hands out. "Here we are. I wanted to share my favorite singer with you."

The marquee said the performer that night was someone named Julien Baker. "I've never heard of him," I said.

"Her. And it's okay. You'll love her."

"How do you know what I'll love?"

"Trust me."

The funny part was, I did. I was losing faith in almost everyone in my life, but I trusted Sloane.

We got to the guy at the entrance, and Sloane handed him two tickets. "Want something to drink?" she asked.

"A beer would be good." We stood in line at the concession stand. "How long have you had those tickets?"

"A while."

I couldn't ask: "Since you just asked me to come to this show today, did you plan on bringing someone else? If so, who, and why am I here instead of them?" The worry that I was an afterthought or a second choice was unbearable, but Sloane didn't make me ask.

"My brother got the tickets because he knows she's my favorite, and he had planned to be here a few days earlier, so we were going to go. I'm actually glad it worked out this way because there's nobody I'd rather be here with than you."

"Oh," I said, and I could feel how red my face was. "I'm glad too."

We got our beers and found a good spot to stand. There was a railing to the left of the stage, and we moved to lean against it so we were off to the side but still in front. We talked until the crowd got so big that it was really loud, and we had to yell. A local band opened for Julien, and they were okay, a little spastic for my taste, but they were decent musicians.

When Julien came onstage, the crowd cheered and then quieted. She stepped up to the microphone and began a sad, dreamy, acoustic song called "Appointments."

I moved close to Sloane's ear and said, "You're right, I love her."

"Just wait." Song after song of deeply emotional, heart-wrenching music ripped at my soul. Finally, the guitar intro of a new song started, and Sloane put an arm around my waist. "This is the song I brought you to hear. 'Shadowboxing.'"

Julien Baker spun a spell around me with the dreamy quality of her voice and the way her songs filled the cracks in my weary soul. I leaned my head on Sloane's shoulder and felt an electric current run through me when she ran her fingers down my spine.

When Julien Baker finished her last curtain call, I hugged Sloane tightly. "Thank you for this."

"You're welcome."

We stepped outside into the muggy air. "Are you hungry?" She looked at her phone. "It's still hours before my car turns back into a pumpkin."

"I'm starving. There's a White Castle down the street."

"I usually save White Castle for the third date."

"Live a little," I said. "Life is too short to play it safe." It felt oddly personal having her words come out of my mouth, and it made me think of other intimacies I wanted to share.

"Touché."

❖

White Castle was packed, but we were finally able to put in our order. "My treat since you got the tickets and drove tonight."

"My brother got the tickets," she said.

"Still, you picked me up, planned the surprise, got us beer. The least I could do is pay you back with a few sliders."

"If it's important to you."

"It is," I said. "There's a table opening up over there in the corner. Do you wanna grab it? I need to use the bathroom." I'd had to pee since shortly after my beer and had been holding it this whole time.

"Sure."

I used the bathroom, careful to squat and came out of the stall to wash my hands. When I looked in the mirror, Clara Braverman stood behind me like something straight out of a horror movie. The slight flicker had increased so that she was flashing like a blacklight at a rave. She'd taken on a bluish hue, and her pupils had expanded so that the whites barely showed. Dry cold seeped into my bones, and I took a step to the side and backed against the wall.

"I need to pass on," she said. "I'm...I'm dying here."

I didn't know what to say to a ghost who felt as if she was dying. "Uh, Mrs. Braverman, I've been trying to figure out why you're still here so I can help you." My voice shook, and I kept having to remind myself that she didn't want to hurt me. Last time, it was an accident.

"And?"

"Well, um...I found the death certificate that confirmed your husband died of heart trouble, but it looks like he filed charges against you in the AfterCorps court which said you were responsible for his death, and that's why you've been going through the hearings and dominion service."

"He *what*?" Now, not only was she flickering, but the lights in the bathroom started to turn off and on. The cold reached my chest, and I struggled to breathe.

"Please stay calm, Mrs. Braverman," I said, struggling to keep my voice smooth. "I want to help you."

"Help me?" She screeched and rushed me, and I realized I couldn't see her legs below the knee; it was as if they'd evaporated, as if she was losing her body as she became less human. "It sounds like you're trying to find ways to make me seem guilty!"

"No, not at all. I just need to figure out why AfterCorps is keeping you here so I know what to do."

Clara stopped an inch from me, grabbed my face, and slammed my head against the wall. The cold and pain was everywhere—my head, my chest, my stomach—I felt as if I'd been dropped into freezing water and couldn't breathe or think or move.

"Fix it!" she screamed. "Fix it!"

I put my hands on top of hers, trying to release her grip on my neck, and the world turned to black.

CHAPTER TWENTY-TWO

I woke up to the sound of a slow, high-pitched beeping and the smell of medicinal sterility. I couldn't open my eyes, but it sounded as if I was in the hospital. Why couldn't I open my eyes?

A door opened, and I heard my mother's voice. "...exactly what I was afraid of, Nathan. You told me she would be safe, and look where we are. Look where your daughter is, just look!"

"You think I wanted this?" Dad said, and it sounded as if he was crying or close to it. "I couldn't control the fact that she had a quickening or that she's an interpreter. It's in her blood. If I could've kept her from this, I would have."

"Oh, you could have. You could have done what I asked."

"I'm the leader of AfterCorps. I was prepared to let our legacy die with me, Joanna. I hoped, right along with you all these years, that Aria would be a reg, and that this would stop with me. But asking me to walk away? Leave AfterCorps with no contingency plan for how they would function in my absence, let this establishment that my great-grandfather built flounder without any kind of guidance—"

"Yes, you chose AfterCorps over Aria, and now our daughter has been attacked by a prior."

The door opened, and someone said, "Mr. and Mrs. Jasper? We have some results back from the tests. Would you like to step out so we can discuss them in my office?"

"Certainly," my dad said.

I waited as long as I could for someone to come back. I didn't want to be alone after what had happened. Every throb of my head brought me back to that bathroom and Clara's fury. She could be here right now, for all I knew, and that thought jolted me. I finally knew exactly how vulnerable I was, and I was terrified. As scared as I was, I was also exhausted. Just listening to my parents' argument had worn me out more than I could have imagined, and sleep won out over fear as I slipped back into the comfort of unconsciousness.

❖

I didn't know how many hours had gone by when I woke again, but I was relieved that this time I could open my eyes. My entire body felt heavy, from the crown of my head to the edges of my toenails. I didn't want to move, so I shifted my eyes to take a look around.

The blinds were slanted open enough that I could see how bright it was outside, and I guessed it was the day after Mrs. Braverman beat me up. I looked to the left and saw my mom. She was asleep in a really uncomfortable-looking position in a recliner that was only about halfway reclined. Her head tilted to the side, her mouth was slightly open, and a tiny snore popped out of her nose. I was so relieved to see her, and I was overwhelmed with love for her and relief at not finding myself alone.

"Mom?" My voice came out as a croak, and I realized how dry my mouth was. I swallowed, and it felt like sand coated my tongue and throat.

I grabbed the sides of the bed and tried to pull myself up. An IV was stuck into my left hand with a tube of clear liquid attached. Slowly, I made it into a sitting position. The room swirled around, and I closed my eyes and swallowed hard.

"Ah, you're awake," a voice said. I jumped, gripped the sides of my bed, opened my eyes, and saw a smiling woman wearing scrubs and a white coat near the end of my bed. My heart slowed when I realized it was just a living, breathing doctor and not a ghost. In the corner, my mom stirred, then jumped to her feet when she saw me.

"Aria!" She rested her hands on my shoulders. "How are you feeling, baby girl?"

"Thirsty." My voice sounded like sandpaper on wood.

"I'll get you some water." She grabbed a giant plastic cup that said "Grant Medical Center" on the side and hurried out the door.

The stranger who'd discovered me awake grabbed a stool from the corner of the small room, wheeled it over, and sat beside me. She looked ready for a serious conversation, and I braced myself. I'd never felt less prepared to discuss anything, but it didn't seem as if I had a choice.

"Ms. Jasper, I'm Dr. Sukul. Has anyone told you why you're here?"

I shook my head.

"Let me fill you in, and maybe when your mother comes back, you'll be able to fill in some blanks for me. Deal?" She had huge brown eyes and stared directly into my eyes as she spoke, and her voice was soft and soothing. I nodded.

"Excellent. You came to us unconscious and nonresponsive after your date found you in the bathroom at White Castle. We've run several tests, everything from blood tests to neurological exams and CT scans, and aside from some bruising and a bump on the back of your head, severe dehydration, and a low body temperature, we've been unable to find anything medically wrong with you. Allowing yourself to become so dehydrated isn't healthy, but it certainly isn't the reason for your collapse and coma."

"Coma?"

"Very short coma," she said, "but yes. We've been unable to wake you for two days."

Two days. I felt sick to my stomach as the room spun, and

the shock of what Dr. Sukul said settled over me. I'd been in a coma for two days after Clara attacked, and I wondered how I would ever be able to be by myself again. Panic clawed at me, and I had to close my eyes and focus on calming my heart and slowing my breathing.

My mother rushed back in with the gigantic cup filled to the top. She'd put a bendy straw in it and positioned the straw at my lips. The water tasted better than anything I'd had to drink in my whole life, and I gulped it down, savoring the coldness and the way it took away the desert feeling that had filled my insides. When I pulled away, half the water was gone from the little jug.

"Better?" Mom pushed my hair behind my ear.

"Lots better," I said, and while my voice didn't sound normal, it was a lot better than the craggy one I'd spoken with a few minutes ago.

"Ms. Jasper." Dr. Sukul rested a hand on my wrist. "What do you remember about the night you collapsed?"

I remembered the concert and going to White Castle. Then I went to the bathroom and...oh.

"I went to a concert with my...with Sloane," I said. "We went to White Castle afterward and I...I was feeling a little dizzy. I went to the bathroom to, you know, splash some water on my face, and I must have fainted."

Dr. Sukul gazed at me for a moment. "You have a significant lump on the back of your head," she said finally. "It's not severe enough to have caused your blackout, but it was cause for some concern. Do you remember how you got it?"

My hand went to my scalp, and I winced when I touched the knot on the back of my head. It was still more than a little tender.

"I must have hit my head when I fell." The lie formed on my lips before I could think twice, and if I hadn't been so traumatized and afraid, I might have worried at how easily I'd begun to hide the truth.

Her eyebrows went up. "I see." She stood and went to the

computer near the doorway, presumably to make some notes in my chart. When she finished, she turned to my mom. "We have a few more tests we're waiting for. If they're clear, I'll be able to let you know when we'll be releasing her. It could be as early as tomorrow if she's feeling okay."

"Really?" Mom asked. "That soon?"

"Yes, provided she's up and walking by then. She'll need to have someone stay with her for several days when she leaves. I assume that won't be a problem?"

"She'll be lucky if I let her out of my sight again before she's thirty," Mom said, and Dr. Sukul laughed when I scowled.

"Very good," she said. "Are you hungry, Ms. Jasper?"

"Starving." Something as normal as eating to cure hunger was exactly what I wanted, and to my relief, Dr. Sukul excused herself after giving me a menu.

❖

"I thought hospital food was supposed to be terrible," I said. I was halfway done scarfing down a cheeseburger and onion rings when I finally paused to take a drink of water.

"It's come a long way since I was in the hospital having you, that's for sure." Mom sat at the end of my bed, her hands wrapped around my feet. She'd spent the half hour from when Dr. Sukul left and I ordered my dinner hugging me, brushing my hair, putting ChapStick on my dry lips, adjusting my pillows, and fussing with my blankets until I finally had to ask her to sit and relax.

"Sorry," she said. "I'm hovering, aren't I?"

"Just a little."

So she'd pulled up a chair by my feet, rested a hand on them, and occupied herself with a book while I rested my eyes. When my food arrived, she set the book down and grinned while she watched me eat.

"I hope your stomach can handle all that," she said.

I swallowed a bite of cheeseburger and said, "The doctor said I could have whatever I wanted."

"Hey, I'm not here to judge. I'm just happy you're well enough to eat." Her smiled faded a little, and when she opened her mouth to speak again, I felt like I knew what was coming. "Aria, what happened?"

In the quiet moments between her making a fuss over me and my food arriving, I'd been preparing myself for this question. As nervous as I was, it was time to come clean about Clara's visits. I'd done myself much more harm than I could've imagined by keeping it a secret.

"I'm going to tell you," I said. "But I only want to tell the story once. Can we wait for Dad?"

She looked like she was going to push it, but she nodded. "I understand. He'll be back first thing in the morning."

I was going to ask her why he wasn't here now when there was a brusque knock at the door. A thin man wearing a wrinkled suit and holding a clipboard came in. "Aria Jasper?"

"That's me." I wiped my mouth and hands and reached up to take his outstretched hand, and I noticed my hand shaking. These sudden sounds and unexpected visitors popping in and out of my room put me on edge, and I wondered again if I'd ever stop being afraid.

"Hi, I'm Gil Peters. Do you have time to answer a few quick questions?"

"What kind of questions?"

He turned to my mother. "Ma'am, could you give us a few minutes? This is standard hospital protocol. I do need privacy with the patient."

"Oh. Okay." Mom squeezed my feet before standing. "I'll go get some coffee."

Gil took the vacated seat and flipped through several pages of different colors. "Tell me about the night you came into the hospital. What were you doing before?"

"I was on a date."

"Okay." He arranged some papers on his clipboard and took notes. "Where did the fella take you?"

"Um. Well, the girl took me to a concert."

His ears turned a little pink, but he didn't look up from his notes. "Go on."

"We saw Julien Baker at the Newport, and when it was over, we went to White Castle. I fainted at the bathroom there."

He nodded at his papers. "Did you sustain any injuries that day or in the days leading up to your collapse that might have contributed to it?"

I thought about my head slamming against the block walls in the bathroom at White Castle. "No, I didn't."

As if he read my mind, he said, "How did you get the bump on the back of your head?"

"I must have hit my head when I fell." While I was ready to tell my parents about what had been happening, I certainly couldn't tell this guy, not unless I wanted to extend my hospital stay. It dawned on me how much interpreters had to lie in order to keep their lives a secret. It wasn't an excuse, but it did partially explain how easy it was for my parents to lead a double life all those years. "It's the only thing I can think of."

Finally, he looked up from his clipboard. "Are you absolutely certain that you don't remember injuring your head in any other way?"

"Yes, I'm sure."

"Ms. Jasper, do you feel safe in your home?"

He knows. They must have specials working in hospitals too. A mixture of panic and relief coursed through me as I wondered how much to tell him.

"You live with your parents?"

I nodded.

"Have you ever been harmed by them, Ms. Jasper?"

"*What?*" I started laughing. "Of course not." My parents had never so much as spanked me.

"Okay, what about your date?"

"Sloane? She'd never hurt me either. Is that what this meeting is about? You think I'm being abused?"

"We take domestic violence very seriously here," he said. "We can make sure you're safe, Ms. Jasper. If you are having any issues with someone in your life, we can get you all the help you'll need."

I felt a moment of sharp disappointment. He wasn't a special sent to help me figure out why Mrs. Braverman was following me, why I could see and talk to her when I hadn't been released yet or how to make her leave me alone and get her crossed over without any further incidents. He was just a reg, here to help me solve a problem I didn't have.

After several minutes of my assurances that I was in no earthly danger from any of my loved ones, Gil Peters handed me a card and left.

❖

My mom returned with coffee for her and a few magazines from the hospital gift shop for me. I was happy to see her, but I was also anxious and uneasy. Soon I'd have to confess to my parents what had been happening to me. I couldn't go on the way I had been, and yet nothing had changed in terms of my reasoning for not telling them. They'd kept so much from me, and even after my quickening had been less than honest about what I should expect. As much as I knew I was in over my head and needed to let them know, there was still the lingering doubt about how much I could trust them.

"Thank you," I said. "Hey, do you happen to have my phone?"

She smiled and crossed to the other side of the room, pulling my phone from a charger on the shelf.

"I know a couple girls who will be very happy to hear from

you," Mom said. "I've been keeping them updated, but I'm sure they'll be glad to know you're able to talk to them yourself."

I had three texts, one from Macy and two from Sloane. The one from Macy said, *Your mom told me what happened. I'm so scared. Please be okay! I love you.* I texted her back that I was awake but tired and would call her tomorrow.

Sloane's first text said, *I can't stop thinking about how pale you were, how scary everything was, how nothing I could do or say would make you wake up. I've only known you a few weeks, and I already don't know what I would do if I lost you.* That one was from three o'clock in the morning, several hours after I fainted. Her other one was from twenty minutes ago. *I heard you're awake!* I texted her back and said I was, and moments later, my phone rang.

"Hello?" I said.

"She lives," Sloane said.

"That she does." I laughed. "How are you?"

"Better than I've been in days." Her voice shook, and I realized it was the first time I'd heard her speak without that little bit of Sloane swagger.

"Yeah, me too," I said. Any time I thought it was impossible to be anything but scared and frustrated, Sloane appeared and changed my mind. I was so touched that she had been affected by what had happened to me.

"Was it her?" She dropped to a whisper. "Mrs. Braverman?"

I glanced at my mom, who was engrossed in her book again. "Yeah."

"That's what I thought. I know you probably can't talk, so just listen. I think it's time we told someone else. My mom or your dad. Preferably your dad. We need to be able to keep you safe."

"I agree." I was glad Sloane felt the same; it confirmed that we'd run out of options and needed to tell someone more knowledgeable.

"You do? Wow, I thought it was going to be a lot harder sell than that. I have two pages of bulleted arguments about why we need to get the big dogs involved."

"I'm sorry about all the extra work." I giggled and realized the last time I'd laughed had been on our date the other night.

"Don't be. Do you want me to be there when you do it?"

"Actually, that would be nice. You're really up for all that?"

"I wouldn't have offered if I wasn't."

I hadn't expected that kind of support, and it made me feel special and honored and so cared for that I could have cried. Sloane's tenderness had a healing effect, and I basked in the warmth that seeped into my bones.

"Okay. Hang on a second." I set my phone down and turned to my mom, who looked up from her book. "What time is Dad coming in the morning?"

"Should be around nine."

"Can you be here around nine?" I asked Sloane.

"Sure." She paused. "Listen, Aria, I found something today. I was back in the file room and I came across…well, I need to tell you about it in person. Maybe we can have a few minutes to ourselves in the morning?"

"I'll see what I can do." Normally, my heart would be racing, and I'd be trying to get her to tell me now, but my eyes were starting to get heavy again. A yawn escaped before I could pop my mouth closed and try to swallow it. "Sorry."

"Rest," she said. "I'll see you tomorrow."

I'd never slept in Sloane's arms, but I drifted off that night with the sound of her voice filled with concern and kindness and imagined she was next to me in my tiny hospital bed.

Chapter Twenty-three

My mom helped me make it to the bathroom early the next morning so I could shower and get into my own clothes before Dad and Sloane arrived. By the time I got back in bed, I was clean and exhausted. I checked the time, and it was only a little after eight. I started flipping through the magazines Mom had picked up, but a few pages in, I fell asleep. A hand on my shoulder woke me.

"Hey, love."

Sloane stood beside the bed, smiling. She had a bouquet of daffodils, and I tried to remember if I'd mentioned they were my favorite flower.

"Hi." I sat up in bed. "Those are beautiful. Thank you." It was so good to see her. I couldn't believe how much I'd missed her over the last few days.

"You're welcome," she said. "Over here okay?" She moved to set the flowers on the side table between the bed and the little lounge chair.

"Perfect."

She pulled a chair over to sit beside my non-IV hand. She kissed it and laced her fingers with mine. The hospital was cold, and I had been wrapped in blankets throughout my stay, but Sloane's hand made heat rise up in me where only a chill had been for days. "Aria, I am so sorry this happened to you."

"It's okay." She was pale, with dark circles under her eyes. I'd been pleased by her concern the night before, but I didn't like the look of her drawn mouth and puffy eyes. I couldn't bear the thought that I was the cause for her being so miserable. "Are you okay?"

"I just…I've been so worried about you. And I feel like this is my fault."

My mouth dropped open. "How could it possibly be your fault?"

"I didn't protect you. I knew the deal with Mrs. Braverman, and I didn't protect you. If I had, I don't know…"

"Followed me into the bathroom when I went to pee, then maybe this wouldn't have happened?"

"Well, yeah."

"No." I took her face in my hand, needing her to know how wrong she was. She and Macy had been the ones seeing me through this madness, and I couldn't allow another moment of her blaming herself for what happened. "You couldn't have stopped it. You can't see or hear Clara. There's nothing you could have done. If you'd asked me if I wanted you to come to the bathroom, I would have told you how ridiculous you were."

A small smile curved one side of her mouth upward. "That sounds about right. Still, I can't stop going over that night in my mind, wondering what I should have done differently."

"Listen." I sat forward and squeezed her hand. "You have nothing to be sorry about. Nothing could have changed what happened with Mrs. Braverman. I think it was inevitable. It's over and done, and I just want to move forward and figure things out. I'm tired of all these secrets. Let's talk to my dad and get everything out in the open."

The last few days in the hospital had given me a lot of time to think about everything that led up to me being there. I had good reason not to trust my parents and had made the best decisions I could based on what I knew, but my situation had gotten too big and too dangerous for me to continue to hide it from them. A cloud of resignation had settled over me when I decided what I had to do. I'd run out of options.

"That sounds good," she said, and the relief in her voice made me sad. She'd been holding my secrets at her own risk. "But, Aria, speaking of your dad and secrets, I need to tell you what I found out." She pulled her hand away and fidgeted with the zipper on her hoodie.

"What is it?"

"I made a copy for you." She reached into her pocket, pulled out a piece of paper folded into fourths, and handed it over. "Read."

I unfolded the page and saw what looked like an article in a newspaper or company newsletter from June 1995. In the center of the page was a blurry black-and-white photograph of a young couple, and from the look of their outfits, they had just gotten married. The picture was fuzzy enough that I had to squint to make out their faces.

"My parents?" I asked, looking up at Sloane.

She nodded.

My eyes returned to the page and I began to read:

> AfterCorps is proud to announce that two of our very own families have merged together in marriage. On June 11, 1995, Joanna Sizemore and Nathan Jasper took their vows at the Columbus Museum of Art.
>
> Nathan Jasper is, of course, the great-grandson of Myron Jasper. He has been an integral part of the organization since he joined in 1988, and took leadership of AfterCorps last year after the death of his father, Art Jasper, to colon cancer.
>
> Joanna Sizemore, known for her roles in La Boheme and Rigoletto at the Metropolitan Opera House in New York City, is the daughter of Fred Sizemore, head of the

CDU. A Columbus native, she spent nine years in NYC pursuing her music career before returning to Ohio upon her engagement.
The Jaspers are honeymooning in Prague.

The paper shook in my hands while I read the article two more times. "I can't believe this."

"I know," said Sloane. "I asked my mom about it. She was kinda surprised I didn't know."

"Why would you have known?"

For the first time, it was her blushing instead of me. "She figured you would've told me."

I closed my eyes and pinched the bridge of my nose. Another secret my parents had kept from me. So far, almost none of the information I'd learned about AfterCorps and my family's involvement in it had come from my mom and dad. Here I was, getting hit with another realization about their lies just as I was planning to share with them my most vulnerable truth. How could I trust these people to do the right thing, to help make sure I wasn't open to another attack? How could I ever trust them with anything again after enduring betrayal on top of betrayal?

A thought pushed through the chaotic fuzz swirling around my mind, and my eyes snapped open. "Two bloodlines," I mumbled. "Your mom said an interpreter would be able to communicate with priors before their release ceremony if they inherited their abilities from two specials but were only protected by one. That has to be why Mrs. Braverman can get through."

"I think so too," she said. "Your grandfather died before you were born, right?"

"Yeah, when my mom was pregnant with me." I gasped. "Didn't Nick say his predecessor was killed on the job by a demonic spirit?"

She took my hand again and squeezed it, and I could tell by the wideness of her eyes that she'd thought of that too.

There was a knock at the door that made me jump, followed

by my mom popping her head in and asking if I was decent. It took everything I had not to ask what she knew about decency. When she saw Sloane, she pulled the door wide enough for she and my father to come in. I blinked back tears when I saw them standing together. Months ago, I knew who I was and who my parents were. I was certain of my past, present, and future. Now I lived in a world where the people who raised me had lied to me my whole life, I'd given up my dreams to talk to angry ghosts, and I was in the hospital because of those two facts.

"Aria?" My dad asked. "What's the matter?"

I handed him the paper, and he held it so he and Mom could both read. It took only seconds for them to exchange a worried look and turn their gazes to me. My mother covered her mouth with her hand.

"How could you keep this from me?" I asked. "And don't tell me you were trying to protect me because you've worn that excuse out, and it's tired. *I'm* tired." Tired didn't even begin to cover it. I felt as if every realization of lie after lie had been piled on top of me, one by one, and I had nearly suffocated from the weight of them. "Tell me the truth."

"Sloane," my father said, "would you mind excusing us—"

"Sloane stays," I said. "She's been the person helping me through all this."

Sloane, who had been rising from the chair, sat back down and squeezed my hand.

"It's time, Nathan," my mother said. Dad sighed. He went to the corner of the room and dragged two folding chairs over so they could sit at the end of my bed. Mom took several deep breaths and began to speak.

"It was my decision to keep you in the dark," she said. "Your father wanted to tell you. He wanted to tell you everything, even when you were a child. He wanted to prepare you to be an interpreter, just as his father prepared him. Just as my own father prepared me, in fact, although I didn't inherit the…" Her lips silently formed several shapes, as if her mouth and brain were having a hard time agreeing on what was the correct word to use. "The ability," she finally said. "I said no. I said no all these years, and I kept on saying it, and your dad went along with it. For me."

The weight on me shifted, and I realized I'd quit breathing. I tried to inhale a big gulp of air, but shallow breaths were all my flattened lungs allowed.

"But why?" I glanced at Sloane, whose eyes were as big as I'd ever seen them. She was as shocked as I was.

Mom closed her eyes for several seconds, and when she opened them again, they were wet with tears. My dad put his arm around her and squeezed her shoulder.

"My father loved being a special. He loved everything about it. He felt fulfilled doing something he thought was so important, and he had a lot of compassion for formers and went out of his way to help them. He began as a field agent and was so good at it, and then worked his way up to the CDU, and that division... it changed him."

"Changed him how?" The warmth I'd felt at Sloane's arrival had been seeping away since I read the newsletter, and the last of it drained from my body with those words from my mother. It was replaced with a frigid chill.

"What do you know about the Criminally Demonic Unit?" Dad asked.

"Practically nothing," I said. "I'm guessing it's the department that handles the really bad formers?"

"No, not formers," my dad said. "Demons have never been human."

"What do you mean?" The chill in my body twisted and churned and felt as if it was becoming something solid inside me.

"I mean, they are demonic forces, spirits that are evil and dangerous."

"Okay," I said slowly. "I guess I thought we were only in the business of ghosts."

"We are in the business of ghosts." His voice sounded

strained. "And it is for the protection of ghosts that we must also be in the business of demons. Look, you've heard of demonic possession, yes?"

"Sure, in horror movies." I was finally getting the truth, and now all I wanted was for everyone to stop talking.

"Well, that happens with the living, but it's very rare. It's much more common for demons to possess formers before they make their final transfer because it's when they're at their most vulnerable. They aren't of this world anymore, and so their souls are beginning to dissipate on this plane, and if a demon is able to take over a former on earth, they can prevent the soul from moving on. And every soul a demon captures makes it that much stronger and harder to deal with."

"And when you say deal with, you mean…?" I didn't want to, but I needed to know. Now that we were finally speaking honestly, I needed to know all of it.

"May I?" Sloane asked.

"Please." My father sounded tired.

"The CDU tracks and hunts demons, and their ultimate responsibility is to destroy them. They use specially designed weapons, the kind that are kept secret from everyone but the highest-level people in the division."

My mom, who'd been staring at the floor, leaned forward and rested her hand on my leg.

"One of those demons killed my dad, your grandpa, two weeks before you were born." I could feel her hand tremble through the thin blankets, and I sat up so I could put my hand on hers. The cold inside me jumped to my chest and formed a lump of dread that made it difficult to breathe. "I just…I never got over it, Aria. And until a few months ago, I put all my energy into letting myself believe that I could bend your future into what I wanted it to be. You're such a talented musician, and I fooled myself into believing that meant you were like me, a normal person with some extraordinary but very human talents. Against your father's better judgment, I got him to agree to go along with my denial."

"I knew better," Dad said. "Don't let your mother think she's the only one to blame. I know I've put you at a disadvantage in your training, and I'm so sorry for that. We're both sorry."

I looked at my mom, tears spilling onto her cheeks, and my dad's gaunt face with dark circles under his eyes. They looked miserable, and I knew they were sorry, which made what I had to tell them even more difficult. I'd been holding this from them out of distrust and anger. Some of that was starting to dissipate—although I knew it would take a long time to repair some of the trust that had been broken—but now I wanted to shield them from what had happened because I knew how deeply hurt they would be.

"The thing is," I began, "it's not just being behind in my training that's the problem. I've been in a lot of danger because of these secrets, and that's why I'm asking you to be honest with me. All of this," I motioned to the hospital room around me, "probably could have been prevented."

"What do you mean?" My dad frowned.

"I've been having a prior visiting me pretty often." I noticed my mom's cheeks getting pale, but I needed to get the words out. "The night I fainted, it was because she approached me in the bathroom and grabbed me."

"Our understanding is that the ward won't work properly if an interpreter receives gifts from both sides of the family but only gets protection from one side," Sloane said, and I was grateful for her input. "We think that must be why Aria was left vulnerable."

"Nathan," my mom whispered.

"No." My dad shook his head vehemently. "No, that's not possible."

"Why not?" I asked.

"Because your grandfather and I forged your protection ward together when your mother was six months pregnant with you."

"What other reason is there for this to be happening to Aria?" Sloane asked. Her grip on my hand had tightened.

My father shook his head once more. "I simply don't know."

Somehow, those words scared me more than anything that had happened so far.

CHAPTER TWENTY-FOUR

I woke up that night in the hospital not knowing what had startled me awake. The doctors had recommended I stay one more night for observation, and even though we all knew my fainting spell had nothing to do with a medical condition, my parents thought it was a good idea, and I agreed to stay.

Now that I was awake again, it shocked me that I'd even gone to sleep at all, given all the drama from earlier in the day. On one hand, I felt as if I was at the beginning of getting my relationship with my parents back. Their confessions about why they'd kept so many secrets didn't erase the fact that they'd lied, and it would be a long road coming back from that, but at least we could start to work on our connection again. On the other hand, we had not solved the reason Clara was able to interact with me. The thought that she could appear anywhere and at any time and nobody knew why or how to fix it was so terrifying that I'd sat awake with the lights on until my eyelids stopped cooperating, and I'd drifted into an uneasy sleep. Images of sinister figures lurking around every corner invaded my dreams.

My room was darker than I remembered it being last night. The now familiar sounds of the hospital—a heart monitor beeping next door, nurses talking in the hallway, doors opening and closing as the staff went in and out of rooms—brought me a little bit of comfort, but I was uneasy. I didn't feel alone. I strained my eyes in the darkness to see if I could make out anything, half expecting to see Mrs. Braverman's gauzy silhouette, or that of a wild-eyed, snarling demon looming over me. The darkness felt stifling, and I fumbled on the panel that controlled my bed position and lighting. I found the button that turned on the light, pressed it, and gasped when the I saw who was in the room with me.

"Nick?" My screech woke him from what looked like a fairly sound sleep, and he jumped out of his chair, then started laughing sheepishly.

"Hey, kiddo," he said.

"You scared the shit out of me!"

He yawned and rubbed his goatee. "I could say the same thing about you."

That was fair, but at least he had known I was in the room with him. My thoughts went to the angry ghost or demon I'd pictured, and I had to pull my blankets tightly around me to ward off that familiar chill of dread. "What are you doing here?"

"Your parents asked me to come. They told me what's been going on with you, and we agreed it's best for you to have an experienced interpreter nearby for the time being."

"Great." I fiddled with the control panel and switched on the dim light above my head so I could turn off the blinding fluorescents.

"Why didn't you tell anyone you were being bothered by a prior?" he asked.

"I did tell someone. Sloane knew."

He rolled his eyes. "So you told someone who's almost as inexperienced as you. Why didn't you tell someone who could actually help?"

"You know how my parents have been. They haven't exactly been forthcoming about all the things I should have known about my life. I didn't have any reason to think they'd be helpful." A shard of guilt stabbed at my stomach, even as I said the words. Because of their secrecy, I'd allowed myself to believe my parents wouldn't have my back when I was in danger. I'd messed up.

"Okay." He nodded. "But what about me? I've been fighting nonstop with your dad to get him to give up the goods so you know what you're getting into. You could have come to me."

"I didn't want to put you in a bad spot." I shivered and pulled my blanket up to my shoulders. It felt as if I'd never escape the fear and unease that caused this chill deep inside. "I wasn't ready to tell my dad, and I didn't want to ask you to keep a secret. I didn't really think you'd keep it from him."

"I would've respected your wishes."

"Really? So if I told you a secret now, you'd keep it between us?"

"I would. I'm your teacher, Aria, and your friend. We've always been cool, haven't we? If you can tell me something that would help me keep you safe, I want to know."

I pulled the blanket more tightly around myself. I needed help, so much more than I'd ever realized. Deep waves of exhaustion washed over me from being afraid and terrorized for so long. "Mrs. Braverman is convinced my father is the one who's keeping her here. She basically thinks he's framed her so she'll be earthbound."

Nick's eyebrows shot up, and those deep grooves returned to his forehead. "For what reason?"

"I don't know. She doesn't seem to know either. She says she's innocent of whatever crimes she's performing dominion service for and says my dad is a bad man who wants to keep her from her final transfer." My discussion with Mom and Dad earlier in the day hadn't lifted any of the heavy weight I carried, but telling Nick about Clara's accusations did.

"And you believe her?" He was studying me carefully.

"I don't know anymore. He's been so secretive, and I got somewhat of an explanation today, but…" I realized I still wasn't convinced about my parents' motivation for secrecy, and that hurt.

"But?"

"I feel like there's still a lot I don't know, a lot they're hiding." I'd wanted today to make me sure of them again, but it hadn't. This might be the jumping point for healing between us, or it might be more deception. My heart ached at the knowledge that I couldn't tell the difference. "Could this be one of the things he doesn't want me to know? I don't believe my dad is the evil leader of a dark empire, but what am I supposed to think right now?"

"How can I help?"

I noticed but didn't mention that he wasn't denying this theory as a possibility. "Can you find out why Clara is still here? It's the only way I'll be able to figure out what's real, and it might get her to leave me alone if I can give her something concrete."

If Clara hadn't attacked me, I probably could have carried her visits myself, only having Sloane and Macy aware of what was happening. I reached to my neck where her hands had wrapped around it and felt the resulting hypothermic-level cold that made a knot in my throat. The deep, freezing pain was as real as it had been the night she assaulted me, and when I closed my eyes, my head thrummed as if Mrs. Braverman was there, slamming it against the wall. I opened my eyes to escape the feelings and images in my head and saw Nick staring at me with concern.

"I'll do my very best," he said. "You have my word."

I slumped a little. Now that I'd shared this information, I felt drained, more tired than I'd ever been. Carrying the secret had worn on me more than I'd realized. I yawned, and a sleepy growl came out of my mouth.

Nick chuckled. "Rest. Let me come up with a game plan, and we will get this figured out."

I put my head back on my pillow, and when I closed my eyes, I forced myself to focus my thoughts on happy things that had nothing to do with ghosts, demons, or AfterCorps. I imagined sitting in my basement with Macy, a bunch of snacks between us and one of our terrible movies on TV. I envisioned myself onstage in front of thousands of people, singing and dancing to the cheers of the audience. Finally, as I began to drift off to sleep, I thought of Sloane's fingers intertwined with mine.

❖

The next day, Nick stepped out of my room while the nurse went over my discharge paperwork and unhooked my IV. I had just dressed in my T-shirt and jeans when I heard a knock at the door.

"You can come on in, Nick," I called.

The door opened, but it was Macy who walked in. I'd never been so happy to see my best friend. My time in the hospital had forced me to think of nothing but my current terrifying situation, and Macy was just the person to counterbalance that. Not only was she the most trustworthy and loyal person I'd ever known, she was also…normal, and just being around her made me feel more normal too.

"Nick was on his cell, but he motioned like I could come in. Do you think he'll let me take you home?"

"I don't know," I said. "I'm kind of on lockdown at the moment; the mature interpreters are taking turns babysitting me."

"I know." When I arched an eyebrow, she shrugged. "Sloane filled me in."

"You two have been talking?" Now both my eyebrows were flexed toward the ceiling. I was surprised they'd gotten close and glad they'd had each other to lean on.

"We've been worried about you."

"Yeah. I've been worried about me too."

"How are you feeling?"

"Physically? Lots better. Still a little sluggish, but another day or two of rest, and it'll be like it never happened as far as my body is concerned. But mentally?" I shook my head. "I'm not really sure how I'm going to get past this." My headache hadn't completely gone away, and there were times it throbbed so badly that it felt as if pain was all that existed. Those moments were becoming more spread apart, though, and the doctors anticipated that they'd stop entirely in the next week. The physical pain was nothing compared to my constant fear that nobody really knew why Clara Braverman was able to talk to me or how to keep me safe from her or any other entity that wanted to harm me.

I'd spent my time in the hospital being numb to what had happened. I'd had strong reactions to discovering my family's history with AfterCorps and the fact that my parents had kept yet another secret from me, but as to what I'd been through—what Clara had put me through—it seemed too much to try to process. But now, with my regular clothes on, preparing to go home and looking into the concerned eyes of my best friend, the reality of it all was starting to flood through me.

"I'm so scared," I said. It was true, but it was also incomplete. My feelings were so vast and deep, I was afraid I might begin to drown in them.

I'd become accustomed to fear that embodied extreme cold, like ice water flowing through my veins or like Clara's deadly grip on my flesh. The new emotion I'd had since waking up this morning was hot. I thought about Mrs. Braverman reaching into me, my being seized with pain and darkness, and my extremities felt hot. The tops of my ears and tips of my fingers and toes burned as if they were being held too close to an open flame. It was a fear born of the knowledge that these events could have been prevented if my parents had chosen, at any point in the last twenty-two years, to tell me the truth about my life. I'd been frightened plenty of times in my life, but that feeling was mixed with another unfamiliar, complex emotion: betrayal.

"What is it?" Macy asked.

"I don't want to go home with my parents," I said. "I can't trust them. But I can't be without them either. I can't risk going through that again without their protection, but how can I depend on safety from people who've let me be so vulnerable?" The reality that my parents had let me down so tremendously that I felt they couldn't keep me safe was devastating. I was beginning to mourn for my relationship with them and feared it would never recover from all of their lies and secrets and misguided efforts.

Macy considered this. "What about Sloane? She's another interpreter, and her mom is experienced, right?"

"Yeah. I don't know if I can ask that of her, though. It would be one thing if Sloane and I had been dating longer and she lived alone, but we haven't fully established what we are to each other. For God's sake, we've been on one date, and you know how that ended. And I don't know how her mom would react to it." I hated that I had become a burden to the people I cared about most. In that moment, I would have run away if I'd thought I could survive on my own. Shit. I couldn't survive on my own, and it gutted me. I went from feeling too full from fear and panic and frustration, to feeling completely and utterly empty.

"There's one way to find out. Wait, what about Nick?"

"What about Nick?" We turned toward the door. He had entered the room without our hearing him.

"Uh, nothing," I said, but Macy was determined.

"Aria doesn't feel comfortable with her parents right now, but she needs to be with an interpreter who can protect her, right? Do you have a couch she can crash on?"

He shook his head. "I'm sorry, I don't."

"It's okay," I said quickly, glancing at Macy with what I hoped was a healthy dose of side-eye. I was embarrassed that she was imposing on him and upset that it truly was my best option. "Really."

"But I do have a spare bedroom you can use."

"Are you serious?" I purposely ignored Macy's triumphant expression.

"Sure, if you want to. I know things with your folks have been rocky, and you're safer with me than probably anyone else right now."

"That's true," I said slowly. "I'm not sure how my parents are going to feel about it." That was a lie. I knew they would be angry and more than a little hurt. It shocked me a bit to realize how satisfying it would be to make them feel as upset as I'd been feeling. "If you're sure, Nick, then I'm in. I'll need to pack some things."

"I'll help you," Macy said.

CHAPTER TWENTY-FIVE

I just don't understand." My mom stood in the doorway to my bedroom, wringing her hands. "Why are you doing this?"

I handed Macy a couple more shirts, and she folded them and stuck them in my suitcase. She was doing an excellent job helping me pack while staying completely out of conversations with my parents.

"I'll be safe at Nick's place," I said.

"You're safe here."

"I need some time away."

"Away from me?"

"And Dad, yeah." Her face crumpled. Any satisfaction I thought I'd get from this was nowhere in sight. I felt horrible, but I knew I was doing the best thing for myself. "I'm not trying to hurt you. It's just…all the deception, all the secrets. I don't feel comfortable with you guys right now."

"We're your parents."

"Mom, just give me time. I love you, and I know you felt justified in what you did, but I can't help feeling like my trust in you is going to take a while to heal."

She opened her mouth, then shut it and walked away. Moments later, I heard her bedroom door slam.

"You okay?" Macy asked.

"I'll be better when we get out of here." I hadn't been

emotional leaving home to go to college, but I was deep in my feelings surrounding moving out like this. I was breaking my mom's heart, and that was almost as unbearable as their bad choices and my broken trust that had gotten me to the point where I felt as if home was no longer a safe place for me.

"I think we've packed everything you need. Ready?"

"Let's go."

❖

Macy followed me to Nick's place in her car. When we got there, she helped me bring in my stuff. The guest room was bright, with a sliding glass door that led to a patio. I stood at the door and looked out in the backyard with its fire pit surrounded by Adirondack chairs and a hot tub on the opposite end of the patio.

"It's nice you have your own bathroom." Macy sat on the blue and gray comforter on the king-size bed. "It kinda seems like this room is the master."

"It is. Nick told me he intentionally took the smaller room with no windows. A lot of his CDU duties keep him out working at night, so he wanted to sleep where it would be dark during the day."

"Lucky for you. Do you want help unpacking?"

"No." I shook my head. "Thanks, though. I think I might actually take a nap." I didn't know whether it was the tension of dealing with my mom, the extreme highs and lows of my emotions in the last few days, or the pulsating pain in my head that had driven me to exhaustion, but I was wiped out.

"It's been an eventful day."

"Yeah, especially considering that I'm still recovering from my Unexplained Fainting Trauma." That was the diagnosis listed on my discharge paperwork. The instructions said I was to have several more days of supervised rest before beginning to return to regular activities.

"Do you want me to stay?" Macy motioned to the recliner in the corner. "That chair looks pretty comfortable, and I have a book in my purse."

"No, you don't need to. Nick is in the next room if I have any trouble."

"Okay. I'll come back tomorrow. Send me a list of snacks. If you're up for it, I can stay over."

I grinned. When Macy didn't know what else to do, she could always be counted on for junk food and good company. I was beyond grateful for her. I appreciated Nick and Sloane for all the ways they were caring for me, but I would have felt really alone after having to distance myself from my parents without her. She'd been a constant in my world since we were practically babies. Right now, when my circumstances had changed so much that I barely recognized my own life anymore, Macy was the person who reminded me who I was and what was real. "I'll text you tomorrow."

She squeezed me in a quick, tight hug and left. I looked around the cheerful room with its pale gray walls and blue and teal accents. It was modern, with streamlined furniture but also cozy with lots of cushy pillows and soft blankets. It felt like as good a place as any to rest, regroup, and make plans for the rest of my life.

A quick double knock at the door gave me hospital flashbacks, and I jumped. A jolt of fear surged through me at not knowing what was on the other side of that door, and I tried to shake it off. *It's just Nick.* "Yeah?"

He popped his head in. "Hey. Just checking to see how you're settling in." He glanced at my suitcase and duffel bag. "Need anything?"

"No, I'm good. I'll unpack a little later. I'm going to nap for a bit."

"Okay. Any requests for dinner? I have stuff to make lentil soup or stuffed peppers. If you want meat, we'll have to make a trip to the grocery store."

I'd forgotten that he was a vegetarian. It would be weird to have a roommate again. I'd only ever lived with my parents and Macy, whom I roomed with at NYU, and I was already used to her idiosyncrasies by the time we moved in together. "Stuffed peppers sound good." I made a mental note to ask Macy to bring some ground beef tomorrow. "Thanks. For everything."

"No thanks needed." He studied me. "You okay?"

"Oh, sure," I said. I tried to smile. "I'm great." I was displaced and lost and sadder than I had ever been, but I didn't want to talk about it.

"I know you're not great, Aria. And it's okay. Rest and heal. Everything else can wait until you get your strength back."

"I'm working on it." As sorry as I was feeling for myself, I knew I was lucky that Nick was allowing me to stay. "Thank you."

He rested his hand on my shoulder, gave it a squeeze, and left the room, softly pulling the door closed behind him.

I pulled a tank top and some soft cotton shorts out of my duffel bag, put them on, and slid between the crisp, cool white and teal checkered sheets. Nick kept his air-conditioning turned up higher than my parents did, and I reached to the end of the bed where the comforter was folded and pulled it up to my shoulders. I'd set my phone on the nightstand, and I grabbed it to tell Sloane I'd made it to Nick's and would talk to her after my nap. The last thing I saw before falling asleep was a text screen filled with x's and o's from her. I smiled even as my eyelids became too heavy to keep open.

❖

I woke up to a tapping sound and sat up, confused about where I was for a moment. I didn't know how long I slept, but the room was dark. The tapping was coming from the right side of the room. I squinted in the darkness and saw a figure standing outside the sliding glass door, and I pulled the blanket around me and shoved myself over so hard I fell off the side of the bed. Panic ripped through me, and I opened my mouth to yell for Nick.

Another tap resonated through the room, and I heard a voice say my name. At first, I thought of Clara Braverman, but why would she be outside? I crawled to the end of the bed to look around the edge.

"Aria, it's me!"

Sloane. I felt silly as I gathered myself up from the floor and went to open the door. I slid it open as quietly as possible to allow her to slip through.

"Sorry I scared you." She sat on the edge of the bed and patted a spot beside her.

"It's okay," I said, sitting next to her. "I've been jumpy since…"

"Yeah. I've been jumpy too, and I didn't go through anything like what happened to you."

"So…what are you doing here?" I asked. "Not that I'm not happy to see you, because of course I am, but why, um, in the middle of the night?" I took a moment to enjoy the way her shaggy hair fell over one eye and how good it felt to have her next to me on the bed. "And why didn't you use the front door?"

She laughed. "First of all, it's barely nine o'clock, so I didn't realize I'd be infringing on the middle of your night. Secondly, I couldn't use the front door because I have a proposition for you that isn't exactly what I would call…Nick-friendly."

"A proposition, huh?" I asked. I realized how close we were sitting. We kept our voices low, and I could feel her breath on my neck when she leaned in to speak, and her fingers intertwined with mine. I wondered how her lips would feel on my neck, my fingers tangled in her wild hair.

She smiled and wrapped an arm around me. "That's not what I meant, but I like where your mind was headed."

The familiar feeling of heat rising to my cheeks made me reach up and touch my face. "Why don't you tell me what you mean, so I don't embarrass myself any further?"

"No embarrassment necessary," she said and leaned in to kiss me. It had been several days since I'd felt her lips, and I was eager to open myself up to them.

The arm she had around my shoulder moved so her fingers were at the nape of my neck and began to trail down my spine as she kissed me more deeply. To my disappointment, she pulled away abruptly. "Listen, before we go any further—and believe me when I say I really want to go further—I need to say what I came here to tell you." She stood and went to the recliner in the corner of the room, dropping down on it. Bitter disappointment filled my mouth, and I swallowed, trying to conceal it.

"I can't be trusted to keep my hands to myself when I'm sitting that close to you," she explained, and I nodded, relieved that I wasn't alone in feeling overwhelmed with desire at being in a bedroom alone. "Anyway, I have an idea, and all I ask is that you give it a real chance."

"Okay. Should I be nervous?"

"No. Well, maybe a little."

"Great," I said, but I couldn't help smiling. My nervous jitters mixed with new adoration for this woman who never tired of coming up with plans to try to help me.

"I've been thinking a lot about this whole thing with Mrs. Braverman and the danger you're in. You can't be under the watchful eye of an experienced interpreter forever, you know? And who knows how long all of this will be going on?"

"It can't be for too much longer," I said. "Now that my dad and especially Nick know what's happening, they'll get it figured out."

"Are you sure about that? What if it turns out they want to keep her here?"

"But why would they want that?" I asked. Sloane looked at her lap. "Do you know something?" For the first time since she'd come in, I wasn't thinking about sex. My pulse rushed so hard I could almost hear it.

"Since you told your parents and Nick about Clara, word has

gotten around AfterCorps about what's happening, and my mom talked to me about it."

"And?"

"And my mom says protocol will probably dictate a new trial for Clara, which could take months if they don't expedite it."

Months? "But...but there's no way they can expect me to be on lockdown for months."

"They might," she said. "And my worry is...look, you're here with Nick, but he's in the next room, just like I was in the next room the last time Clara came at you. Granted, I wouldn't have been able to do much, and Nick can, but I also had no idea anything was happening to you. You could be in a lot of danger in the seconds or minutes it takes to get to you, and it could be worse this time."

"What are you suggesting, that Nick never leave me in a room by myself?" I thought the weight of all the changes and disappointments and lost trust had been suffocating, but that would be no comparison to having to be under that kind of watch. The thought alone made the air in the room turn thick and difficult to inhale. "Because that's no way to live, Sloane. Especially not if we are talking about months." I had to draw a line somewhere, and constant in-room supervision was where I was doing it. The slow loss of control over my life had made me feel powerless and frustrated beyond measure, but this? This I could control, and I didn't care at what cost it came. I would not give up my privacy, the base level of quality of life.

"No, I'm suggesting something a little more radical than that." She sat on the floor at my feet. She took my hands and looked into my eyes. I felt a blush coming on, but she dropped the bomb she'd been holding, and all flirtatious thoughts left me. "I think you and I should cross Clara over."

"*What?*"

"Let me explain. I know I can figure out how to do it. Before they had a designated person in charge of final transfers, it used to be a rotating responsibility. Everyone had to spend three months every two years on that job, so there are books on it. They keep a set of archived books in the storage room where we did our filing, so all I have to do is get back in there."

"That's so far from all you have to do," I said. We'd encountered a lot of incidental danger, stuff beyond our control, and that was one thing, but what she suggested would deliberately push us into harm's crosshairs.

"Yeah, it would take some sneaking in on our part. We'd have to figure out people's schedules and stuff, but it's a plausible plan."

"Plausible? Sloane, have you even thought about what kind of punishment there would be if we managed to accomplish this? Clara would be gone; there would be no way to hide it. People would find out it was us, and then where would we be? There's a good possibility we would be kicked out of AfterCorps for good." I was surprised to realize I didn't want to get kicked out. When had I stopped wanting to run away from ghost training and the organization that had a hold on me?

Her grip on my hands tightened. "I can't lose you, Aria."

"You're not going to lose me."

"I might." To my surprise, her eyes filled with tears. She blinked hard and shook her head. "You don't know what it's been like watching you go through this and feeling so helpless. I need to do something, do you understand? I have to fix this somehow."

I looked into her eyes. They were silvery with the remains of a few tears, and her eyebrows were drawn and furrowed. She had never been more beautiful. I was moved by her concern for me, and understood that her desire to find a way to get me out of this situation and back to safety was the origin for her crazy plan.

"Come here," I said softly, tugging on her hands. "Please."

She got on the bed. I leaned in and kissed her. She tensed with surprise before she pushed deeply into my mouth with her tongue and put her hand on the back of my head. We tipped back, and our mouths began traveling each other's bodies. Her lips grazed down my neck, opening when she reached my collarbone.

I closed my eyes when I felt her tongue trace the delicate skin. I inhaled deeply and smelled the fresh citrus scent of her shampoo.

When her mouth returned to mine, I slipped my hand inside her shirt and grazed her belly and moved up her side. She gasped and grabbed my hand.

"Aria," she whispered, "are you sure? You just got out of the hospital. Are you sure this is okay?"

"Yes," I whispered and nibbled on her bottom lip. "I've never been so sure." This was the kind of danger I wanted, the kind that didn't scare me, the kind that felt so good.

She slipped a strap of my tank top to the side, dropping kisses across my shoulder as she slid it down my arm. Her mouth moved lower on my chest, and she yanked the top off, and my nipple was in her mouth. She licked in a circular motion, and when I felt her teeth graze across it, I grabbed a handful of her hair.

She moved down my body, her tongue and teeth finding sensitive parts of my stomach until she got to the edge of my pants, just below my navel. She lingered, pulling the fabric down slowly, almost lazily, as if she were in no hurry at all. Each time she moved my waistband a fraction of an inch, she replaced the fabric with her lips. Finally, she put her hands under my hips and lifted them so she could pull my pants off. She stood at the end of the bed, and in the darkness, I saw her slip off her T-shirt and shorts.

Once there was nothing between us, she rushed to the center of me, her slow deliberation from moments before replaced with divine urgency. She spread my thighs apart, and when I felt her mouth on my clit, I had to press my face into a pillow to stifle a moan. I arched my back and pulled my legs toward me so she could have all of me and was rewarded with her fingers slipping inside.

We matched each other's speed, me rocking my hips to the motion of her tongue and fingers. I raked her hair, pushing harder against her tongue as my entire body began to vibrate.

She became more forceful with her fingers, and seconds later, an intense orgasm quaked through me.

She crawled to me, kissing her way back up my body. We found our way to each other's mouths again.

"You feel amazing." I cupped her breast and ran my thumb over her nipple, enjoying her gasping into my mouth. "I want to taste you, Sloane."

She bit my bottom lip and pressed her body against mine before pulling away. She grabbed my hips again, this time to pull me down the bed, then she straddled my head, grabbed the headboard, and lowered herself to my mouth.

I took her into my mouth, sucking and licking at the same time. She tasted sweet and salty, like the air when you stand near the ocean. My tongue swirled on her clit, and she ground against it, pushing against me so hard I could barely breathe and didn't want to. I grabbed her hips and guided her to my mouth, over and over, until I felt her body clench and shatter.

She collapsed beside me and pulled me close.

"Well," she said, "this isn't the reason I came here tonight. Not that I'm complaining, of course." She kissed my cheek and trailed her fingers across my shoulder. "This was incredible."

"It was." The moon was almost full, and it seemed low and close tonight. Some of its soft light swathed Sloane's face, and her eyes looked like a shock of lightning across a dark sky.

"Aria?"

"Yeah?"

"I love you."

I sat up and stared. "You do?" She had the ability to surprise me in a way that healed the sting of all the other bad surprises I'd endured.

"Yes, I do." She sat up too, and I realized how embarrassed she looked. I needed to respond before she thought I didn't share her feelings.

"I love you too." I took her hand. "I've actually never said that before. To a girlfriend, I mean." I'd never even come close to love before, partly because I was always too busy singing to get too deeply involved with anyone, and partly because it had seemed such a daunting thing. Somehow with Sloane, it felt right and natural.

She smiled. "Well. Here we are, then. Loving each other."

I laughed. "Here we definitely are."

We lay back down, facing each other, smiling. When Sloane's expression darkened, I touched her cheek. "What is it?"

"This is why I can't lose you." She pulled my hand from her face and laced her fingers into mine.

I sighed. "Sloane—"

"I know. I know you think it's crazy. All I'm asking is that you think about it." Her eyes were so dark and wide, and she gripped my hand so tightly. Her fear was palpable, and in that instant, I would have done anything to keep her from worrying about losing me anymore.

"Okay," I said. "I can't promise I'm ever going to agree with you, but I'll think about it, and we can talk about it some more. But not tonight, okay?"

"Deal. Not tonight."

We settled into the bed together. She fell asleep in minutes, but it took me longer to relax. For one thing, it finally registered that all this had happened at Nick's house, and I felt weird about having Sloane in my bed when I was his guest. For another, I couldn't stop turning her plan over in my head. She hadn't gone too deeply into the logistics, and I considered what they might be until my vision wavered, and my brain was cloudy. When I finally allowed my eyes to close, it was only moments before my drowsiness overtook me. I fell asleep in Sloane's arms for the first time.

CHAPTER TWENTY-SIX

A knock at my door the next morning jolted me from a deep sleep. I looked beside me, and the space was vacant. Frowning, I pulled the covers to my chin and yelled, "Come in."

Nick poked his head in the door. "Hey, we need groceries. How soon can you be ready?"

"I'll need to shower and get dressed. Twenty minutes?"

He nodded and popped out.

I let the blankets drop down on the bed and got up, crossed over to the sliding glass door, and peeked through the blinds. The yard was empty. Grateful as I was not to have been caught in an embarrassing situation with my girlfriend, I didn't like the hollow feeling in my chest that came with the realization that Sloane had crept out in the night.

"Good morning, babe," said a quiet voice behind me, and I jumped and whirled around.

Sloane came out of the bathroom wrapped in a towel, her hair still wet from a shower. It took me about a second and a half to remember that I was still naked, and I bolted to the bed and grabbed the comforter to wrap around myself. She smiled, and I knew she was remembering last night, when there wasn't a shred of fabric covering either of us, but she didn't say anything. I was relieved for her slow, nonchalant manner since last night had been so unexpected. She didn't seem embarrassed or freaked out; in fact, she seemed even more laid back than normal, which set me at ease too.

"I heard Nick," she said, keeping her voice low. "I'll get dressed and slip out of here, okay?"

"Sounds good. Macy is coming over later if you want to come back and hang out this afternoon."

"Yeah, I might do that. Text me when she's here, and let me know if you still want me to come back." She leaned in to kiss me, and water from her hair dropped onto my temple and rolled down my cheek.

Another, louder knock came at the door, and Sloane rolled off the bed and onto the floor so she was hidden in case Nick popped back in. I pulled the comforter tightly around me and told him he could come in.

"Here's the grocery list I made so far." He strode over and put a small pink sheet of paper on the nightstand. "Look it over and add whatever you want."

"Okay, thanks." I picked it up and pretended to read it.

Nick walked back to the door. On his way out, he paused. "Sloane, you can come grocery shopping with us too, if you want."

❖

She did come with us after Nick waved off my embarrassed, stuttering apologies for having a girl in my room overnight without running it past him. "You're a grown woman, and I have no interest in policing your personal life. You're with me for your safety, and that's all." Macy met us at the store to pick out carnivorous snacks before heading back to Nick's place.

"Do you need me to run to my house to cook this?" Macy asked Nick, holding up a container of ground beef.

He laughed. "No, I'll fire up the grill for you. Know how to use one?"

"What do you think I am, an amateur?"

"I did, and now I know otherwise." Nick went out the side door from the kitchen and pulled a cover off an enormous charcoal grill. Macy started forming the ground beef into patties, and Sloane and I chopped up veggies for stir fry. We'd all slipped into our duties, and as I looked around, I saw that, albeit temporary, this was my new home, and these people loved me. This was as much a family as the one I'd grown up in, and I was overcome with gratitude.

The open floor plan allowed us to see into the living room from the kitchen, and Nick had turned on a show I didn't recognize.

"Nick, what is this?" I asked when he came back inside.

"Are you serious?" He looked at each of our faces, and when he saw that none of us were familiar with the program, he shook his head. "You kids today don't even know what you're missing. You don't know Columbo when you see him. Guys, this is one of the best procedural crime dramas of all time. The detective seems like this bumbling, absentminded nincompoop, but he's actually smarter than everyone and always solves the mystery in less than an hour."

He sat on the edge of his couch, leaned forward, and clasped his hands together, and it was a posture I was accustomed to seeing when he and my dad watched basketball. I hadn't realized his television passions extended to '80s detective shows. I glanced at Sloane and smiled, and a slow movement on the far side of the living room caught my eye.

Clara Braverman stood in the corner, gently waving at me.

At first I didn't believe what I was seeing. I blinked and looked away, but Clara was still there. Panic and terror took over, and a familiar cold began in my fingers and traveled to my throat so quickly that I nearly choked on it. Pain seared through my hand, and when I looked down, I saw that I'd sliced myself with the knife I'd been using to cut zucchini. Sloane must have noticed because seconds later, she was at my side with a hand towel.

"Shit, you're bleeding a lot." She wrapped the towel tightly between my finger and thumb where a steady flow of blood streamed out. Once she'd completed her bandage, she raised my hand in the air. "You need to sit down and keep this above your heart." I let her hold my hand in the air, but my body hadn't even recognized any physical pain. All I could feel was the icy freeze that had taken over my entire torso, like a frigid wave of terror had made a home in me.

"What happened?" Macy and Nick asked, almost in unison.

"She cut herself," Sloane said, guiding me over to the chair next to Nick. I couldn't move my eyes away from the corner of the room where Clara stood, motionless and solemn.

"She's here," I said, allowing Sloane to settle me into the chair. "Mrs. Braverman, she's right over there."

Nick, who'd been focused on my hand, turned to the corner, stood, and approached Clara. "What is it you want?"

"I want to leave this place." Her voice sounded garbled, as if she were speaking under water.

"We're working on that," he said.

Clara shook her head. "He won't let me go." She pointed at me. "Her father won't let me leave. I can't rest. I can't rest. I'll never rest. I'll never let her rest." Her voice had gone from low and gurgling to high and shrieking. She turned and faced me, her arm still outstretched. "You won't have a peaceful night of sleep until I transfer. Tell that to your daddy."

Nick moved between Clara and me, murmuring something I couldn't distinguish, and when he turned around, she was gone.

CHAPTER TWENTY-SEVEN

W hat the hell just happened?" Macy wailed.
Sloane, who had been standing behind me with her hands on my shoulders, was now sitting next to me. We huddled together, trying to regain warmth we'd lost being so close to Clara. The couch trembled, and I began to realize how violently we were shivering. Nick had made her go away somehow, but not before she could threaten me. He'd made her go away, but he hadn't been able to keep her from appearing. Could he keep her from making good on her threat? Frightened thoughts ricocheted off the edges of my aching head.

"The prior was here," Nick said, rummaging through a cabinet in the kitchen. "She's gone now." He found whatever he was looking for and came to stand in front of Sloane and me.

"Open your mouth," he said. I looked at him, not completely comprehending what he wanted me to do. He held up a thermometer in front of my face. "Mouth. Open." I did as he asked and slowly closed my mouth around the device. When it beeped and he pulled it out to examine the electronic window, he shook his head and moved to shove it in Sloane's open mouth.

"Macy, go to the bedrooms, grab all the blankets off the beds, and bring them in here." He was only halfway done with his sentence before Macy ran down the hallway. She came back with her arms full of quilts and comforters and began wrapping us up. My attempts at trying to make sense of what had happened gave way as the cold consumed me. I'd had several moments where I felt I was just keeping my head above the suffocating freeze that occurred when Clara came around, but now, against my will, I succumbed to it. My heartbeat slowed, and my mind went blank, and all that existed was the glacier that lived in my body.

"What's going on?" she asked.

"Their temperatures are just barely above ninety-five degrees. That's almost hypothermia. We have to get their body temps back up. Macy, sit here beside Aria. I'll get next to Sloane. Sit as close to her as you can, with as much of your body next to her as you can manage. They need our heat."

"Why are they so cold when she was only here for a minute?" Macy asked. "Sloane told me it would take extreme contact for Aria to have such a bad reaction."

"The longer Clara is earthbound, the worse their reactions to her will be."

I wasn't sure how much time had gone by when I felt Sloane shift. I turned my head, and she was staring at me with tears in her eyes.

"Are you okay?" Her words were careful and slow.

It took several seconds for my lips to form the words I wanted to say. "I think so. Are you?"

"Yeah. I think so."

"Can you walk?" Nick asked. "We'll help you up."

"Where are they going?" Macy asked.

"I think the best thing is to get them into bed. We can cover them in blankets, and if they're together, their body heat will gradually rise."

Macy and Nick leaned down, each putting an arm around my waist, and helped me to stand. I hobbled down the hallway between them, stumbling as if I were drunk, and let them lay me down in the bed. On the edges of my periphery, I registered some alarm that I couldn't feel my extremities, but I didn't have the clarity to worry about it further. Macy ran back to the living room and returned with the blankets that had covered me on the couch. They left, and just when I was starting to think they'd changed their minds about bringing Sloane to the bedroom, they came back, and Sloane tumbled onto the bed beside me. While Macy got us covered in blankets, Nick hovered over us.

"Sloane, where's your phone?" he asked. "I have to call your mom and tell her you're staying here tonight."

Sloane rocked toward me a little and felt in her pocket. She handed Nick her phone.

"It's locked," he said. "Can you remember your code?"

"Zero, three, two, seven," Sloane mumbled.

I'd been close to falling asleep when I heard those numbers, and the smallest touch of warmth filtered through my heart. March twenty-seventh was my birthday. I searched my memory, trying to think if I had told Sloane my birthday, but I couldn't seem to remember any of our specific conversations, nor could I build up the energy to ask her about it. I closed my eyes and smiled. My birthday.

I heard Nick speaking to Sloane's mom in the hallway before I let sleep overtake me. I had dreams about being alone in Nick's empty apartment and Clara coming to hover over me, to threaten and hurt me again.

❖

The smell of bacon and eggs woke me, and when I opened my eyes, I saw Macy and Nick, each with a tray of food. Sloane stirred and sat up, rubbing her eyes, and I scooted up so I could lean against my pillows.

"Good morning." Macy brought a tray, set it on my lap, and sat on the edge of the bed near my feet. Nick got Sloane situated with her food and then settled into the recliner in the corner of the room.

My fingers felt a little stiff, and I rubbed my hands together like I would if I was outside in the winter, getting the blood flow going. I didn't feel cold, but I had pins and needles in my hands and feet. When it had subsided a little, I picked up my fork and ate a bite of eggs. It felt strange to be doing something so ordinary as eating breakfast after going through something so traumatizing, but I tried to focus on the taste, feel, and texture of the food, afraid that even thinking too much about Clara would bring back that heart-stopping freeze.

"Nick even made you bacon," Macy said. "I told him he didn't have to, that we could give you eggs and fruit, but he insisted."

"You need a hearty breakfast," he said. "You went through a lot yesterday, and it all went down before dinner." He smiled at his joke, but his lips were thin.

"Thank you," I said. "For everything." I took a large bite of bacon to show my appreciation.

Sloane took a big swallow of orange juice and cleared her throat. "Yeah, thank you," she said. Then, after a pause, "Nick, what are you doing to make sure this doesn't happen again?"

"Sloane—" I began.

"No, I'm serious. How many times does Aria have to get hurt for someone to do something about it?"

I loved her for asking, for her anger and indignance.

He leaned back in his chair and crossed one leg over the other. "You both got hurt this time."

"I wasn't the target, and you know it."

"What do you think should be done?" I couldn't interpret the look on his face. Bemused, maybe, with a touch of solemnity. I didn't appreciate that he didn't appear to be taking this seriously, and like Sloane, I wondered what terrible thing would have to happen to me in order for him to take notice. Maybe he'd care when I was dead and he had facilitated my transfer.

"We have to get Clara transferred," Sloane said. "It's the only way she'll leave Aria alone."

"I'm working on that."

"How?"

"You need to trust me."

I scoffed at this and crossed my arms when Nick raised an eyebrow. The time when I'd blindly trusted the people in my life was long gone.

Sloane pushed her tray away as well as she could with its legs tangled in her blanket. "That's not good enough. It's gone too far, Nick. I want a plan, I want answers, and Aria needs them. She deserves that." This was the reason loving Sloane had come so easily.

Nick sighed and closed his eyes for a moment. When he opened them, his gaze was pointed. "You're right. I didn't want to discuss it until the investigation had given me substantial results, but you're right." He turned to me. "After everything that's happened, Aria, you have earned some answers that haven't been filtered through a misguided attempt to protect you from your own life.

"I, along with a few other AfterCorps leaders, have begun an internal inquiry because we suspect that Clara may be right and that your dad might be keeping her here against her will without cause. And not only her, I'm afraid. There may be as many as a dozen or so others."

"But...but why?" I hadn't realized I was trembling until I felt Macy rest her hand on my shin and squeeze. Throughout all I'd endured, I hadn't really been able to bring myself to believe my dad was capable of something like this, even on my worst days. This couldn't be real.

"What motivation could he possibly have to sabotage priors to whom he feels such a deep responsibility?" Sloane reached under my blanket to find my hand. "Not to mention the business his family built over multiple generations."

"We aren't sure about that yet," Nick admitted. "That's the main reason I've held off telling you; we aren't positive about his reasoning, although we do have some theories."

"Like?" Sloane sounded more impatient than ever, and I

squeezed her hand. I was as ready as she was to hear what Nick had to say, but I couldn't seem to find my voice.

"How much do you know about your father's financial situation, Aria?"

"Practically nothing." I couldn't imagine what his finances had to do with anything. My parents had always lived comfortably. Not extravagantly but definitely comfortable. I couldn't remember a time I'd wanted or needed anything they couldn't provide. But that didn't really answer the question, did it?

"Well, here's a condensed breakdown: AfterCorps was built so that surface jobs could fund the work we do. That work has gotten progressively more expensive because of the ways we operate now. Industrial and technological advances have simplified and streamlined a lot of our jobs, but it comes at a hefty cost.

"In short, your parents have had more money going out than coming in for quite some time, and I don't envision that changing any time soon. It would be more cost effective for Nathan to get AfterCorps to implode than it would for him to keep it going. He could then just focus on the funeral business and get the money to roll back toward his bank account."

My dad had spoken of AfterCorps with so much pride and reverence. I thought about my parents arguing when I was in the hospital and how my dad hadn't walked away from this organization no matter how much my mom had wanted him to. He'd been so concerned about how AfterCorps would survive if he left, I couldn't make sense of a scenario in which he would purposely sabotage it. And that didn't even begin to explain how he was suddenly okay with putting his only daughter at risk of harm and death.

"Wait a minute," Macy said. "I get that I know the least about AfterCorps of anyone in this room, but I know Aria's parents. Even if they wanted all this to go down like you say, there's no way they'd jeopardize Aria's safety to make it happen." *Thank you, Macy.*

"Which explains why they were so disproportionately devastated when Aria had her quickening, and why they have been acting so strangely since she began her training." He uncrossed his legs and leaned forward. "Don't you think it's odd that they have dismissed what you're doing in AfterCorps and kept you in the dark about everything from your lineage to basic interpreter protocol? It seems like they don't think you'll have to worry about being an interpreter for very long, and if the goal is to run AfterCorps into the ground, they would be correct."

I slumped back on my pillows and looked at the remains of my cold eggs. How could this be happening? Part of me felt there was no way my father would sacrifice his integrity along with everything his family had ever worked for to plan something like this. Another part had to acknowledge that this was the most plausible thing I'd heard since I'd come into my interpreter abilities. I didn't want any part of this to be true, but I owed it to all of us to consider it.

"What happens if AfterCorps is destroyed?" I asked.

"Everything would change for the dead and the living. There would probably be clusters of people helping priors transfer, but it would be unorganized. Chaos. There'd be no judicial system, no way to track anything. It would be interpreters helping ghosts cross over who had no business moving on to their last destination. And a lot of priors would slip through the cracks and wander the earth indefinitely."

I couldn't wrap my mind around that, nor could I fathom that my father was capable of torturing Clara. The lying I'd accepted, but this? It would make my dad a monster, and that I couldn't accept.

"What can we do?" Sloane asked.

"The best thing the two of you can do is stay here where I can protect you. Sloane, I've told your mom I'd like to have you stay with me. She knows about Aria's situation, of course, and I let her know we are going to have training here because it's too dangerous to try to transport her back and forth. I said we'd be doing intensive training, a bootcamp of sorts. She'll be bringing some clothes by for you later."

Sloane nodded slowly.

"What if…" I swallowed hard. "What if all this is true? What will happen to my father?" I was terribly torn between desperately needing and completely not wanting the answer.

Those deep grooves appeared on Nick's forehead, and he frowned. "I don't know." That was a lie, though. He did know, and the fact that he didn't want to tell me made me more frightened than I'd ever been.

CHAPTER TWENTY-EIGHT

It'll take a day or two to regain your strength," Nick said, shuffling Macy toward the door amidst her promises to text to check on us later. "I'll be in the next room, so yell if you need me."

I lay down and wondered if I'd actually be able to sleep with all these disturbing thoughts occupying my mind.

"What are you thinking?" Sloane asked.

"That my life is a castle of lies built on a foundation of deceit," I said.

"Dramatic," she said, but her voice was gentle, and she stroked my arm and shoulder.

"You asked."

"I did."

"Sloane?"

"Yeah?"

"Do you think there's still a way to figure out how to transfer Clara even if we aren't doing our training at AfterCorps?"

She drew herself up onto her elbow and stared. "Well, yes. There's always the sneaking out option. Although I'd have to go alone; it's too dangerous for you. At least I know if I'm by myself, priors can't come at me."

"Okay. Think you could do it tomorrow night?"

"I don't see why not unless I unexpectedly take a turn for the worse." She grabbed my hand. "Are you sure?"

"I think so. This investigation could go on a while, and there's no guarantee this was the last we'll see of Clara. In fact, it's practically guaranteed that she will come back. Besides, if Nick is right, what's the point in trying to preserve good standing for either of us at AfterCorps? If my father succeeds, there'll be nothing left. If he fails…well, I think they'll have bigger fish to fry than a few unruly trainees who took matters into their own hands."

The words came out in a jumbled rush, I was so afraid of having second thoughts or taking time to think too hard about what it meant to admit that my father might be behind everything that had happened to me. Feelings had become too dangerous, and I was ready for action.

"You're really serious, aren't you?"

I bit my lip hard before answering her. "I am."

❖

We tossed around the possibility of letting Nick in on what we wanted to do, but in the end, decided against it. While he'd finally opened up about the investigation, it had been a challenge to get him to that point, and he'd been less forthcoming about the details. He'd also rebuffed Sloane's attempts to get him to see how dire it was to get Clara to cross over as quickly as possible, and since that was our goal, it seemed better not to tell him. The truth was, I fully trusted only two people now: Sloane and Macy. As much as I appreciated everything Nick had done for me, I wasn't convinced about his intentions.

Our plan was pretty straightforward. Sloane's mom would come to bring her clothes, and Sloane would distract her with a tour of Nick's place while I went through her purse to get her AfterCorps badge. With it, Sloane could later gain access to where she needed to go.

"My mom lost her badge once before," she explained when she got the text that her mom was on the way. "It took forty-eight hours before they could issue her a new one because that's how long an old one is active when it's reported missing. I guess enough people have lost them and then found them in their houses or whatever a day or two later, so the rule was instituted to save money."

"Kinda speaks to some cash flow problems, doesn't it?" I shook my head when I saw the concern in Sloane's eyes. "I'm okay. Just ready to get this over with." My nerves had become thin and worn, and all I wanted was to get out of my current state and move forward with my life. I was barely fazed by the risk involved anymore.

Sandy Dennison arrived with a duffel bag slung over her right shoulder and a purse clutched in her right hand. Sloane hugged her mother for a long time, then grabbed the duffel bag, along with the purse, and took them to the bedroom. When she came back, she had Nick with her.

"Hey, Mom, you should see Nick's herb garden in the back."

"Oh, really? Nick, I didn't know you had a green thumb."

"I dabble a little." He smiled. "Come on out. I'll show you."

Sloane stepped outside with them but not before nodding toward the bedroom where I was already headed.

The purse was on top of the duffel bag in the center of the bed. I reached in and found her wallet. When I pulled it out, her keys came with it and clattered to the floor.

"Shit." I paused to make sure the sound hadn't alerted anyone to come see what I was doing, but based on the total silence, I guessed they were still outside. The keys went under the bed, and I had to move the dust ruffle to find them. Once I got them back into the purse, I started going through the wallet. There were photos of Sloane and her brother as kids and what looked like senior pictures. My fingers shook as I flipped through the different compartments: driver's license, debit card, credit cards, reward cards for gas stations and grocery stores. I'd searched every section and hadn't found it, and I heard a door close.

"It's just lovely," Sandy said.

I shoved my hand into the purse and got stuck in a small side pocket. I felt something cold and plastic—the AfterCorps badge. I jammed the wallet back into the purse and stuck the badge in my pocket just in time to hear Nick coming down the hall.

"You hungry?" he asked, filling the doorway. "I've had a stew cooking in the Crock-Pot all day, I figured Sandy might want to sit down for a meal with us."

I hoped the guilt I felt about adding thievery to the list of things I'd done to try to free myself of Clara didn't show on my face. "I could eat," I said. "Let me just wash my hands first."

❖

"Are you sure you don't want me to come with you?"

I was watching Sloane, dressed all in black, put on her backpack. We'd packed her mom's badge, my keys to the outer funeral home doors, a can of mace, and a flashlight. She wouldn't need the backpack just for those small items, but we wanted to give her a way to carry back any helpful papers or items that would get us closer to learning how to get Clara crossed over.

"You know you can't." She sat beside me on the bed. "Look, I know you're worried, but this is how we have to do it. Believe me, I'd much rather have you come with me, but we can't take the risk."

"Just be careful." We stood and hugged. I held her as tightly as I could before releasing her. "I love you." I had new respect for what she had been through since we'd been together. I hadn't fully appreciated how worried she'd been until now, when I wanted to go and protect her and keep her from going into danger without me. She'd become such a big part of my world in these few short weeks, and I couldn't handle the thought of anything happening to her.

"I love you too. I'll text when I'm there."

She grabbed her car keys off the nightstand and slipped out the glass door. Once outside, she gave me a quick wave before disappearing into the night.

❖

I'd been pacing for almost two hours when I heard the door open. I whirled around and saw Sloane creeping in. I'd gotten the text that she was in the office and another telling me she was on her way back, but I'd gotten no other details. It had been the longest two hours of my life, worrying about whether she was okay, wondering what I'd say to Nick if he came in to check on us and discovered she was gone, and burdened with the nearly uncontrollable fear that Mrs. Braverman would come back while I was alone and defenseless.

I rushed to her and gave her a hug, and she kissed my cheek. When she pulled back, she dropped her backpack, and it sounded heavier than when she left. She moved slowly across the room and sat gingerly on the bed.

"Well?" I asked.

"I think I found what we need. I got some textbooks. I didn't take the time to read them. I just grabbed what I found and got out of there."

Something about the quiet, careful way she spoke set me on edge. "What is it?"

She was silent so long, staring at the floor, that I started to think she wasn't going to answer. Finally, she raised her head, and I saw how pale her skin was, how dark her eyes. "Clara was there."

"You *saw* her?" I gasped. "But...but how?"

"Come sit with me."

Dazed, I sat next to her. She swallowed hard before she began to speak. "I was in the storage room looking for the books. I heard someone behind me or maybe just felt them, and

I thought, 'That's it, I'm caught.' Because a lot of AfterCorps business happens at night, and I had a story in case I bumped into anyone, but I didn't have any way to explain why I was creeping around the storage area.

"Anyway, it was her. She looked a lot different from when she came here, Aria. She looked…brighter, more substantial."

"But if there were no other interpreters around, you shouldn't have been able to see her." This had to be a mistake, and if it wasn't, my world was about to get rocked again. My mouth went dry, and I could barely swallow.

"I know." She nodded impatiently. "Just listen. She was terrified, kept looking behind her, and she talked so fast." She scrubbed her eyes and shook her head as if to clear it. "Clara said she's being possessed by a demon. She's trying to fight it, but she's losing. She said the last two times she came to you, she wasn't the one in control. The demon is coming after you."

That warm heat crept into me again. Sweat prickled my temples, and my neck and chest flushed. Since I'd learned about my grandfather having been killed by a demon, there hadn't been any more talk about them, and after a couple tense days in which I imagined frothing-mouthed demons coming for me in the dark, I'd put my thoughts about them aside. Clara had seemed the more pressing threat. I had no idea I'd left myself open to the real danger.

"Do you believe her?" I asked. "Do you think it's true?"

"Yes, I do."

I jumped up. "We have to tell Nick. If it's true, it's so much more dangerous than any of us thought."

Sloane stood and grabbed my hands. "We can't tell him."

I gaped at her. "Why not?"

"Because Nick is working with the demon. It's not your father that's behind Mrs. Braverman being stuck here. It's Nick."

Just like that, this whole swirling, fuzzy mess of circumstances began to come into focus and sharpen. I was living in the home of the man responsible for demonic attacks on me, and we'd very nearly told him we were going to try to force Clara's transfer. My father wasn't behind it; Nick was. I trusted Sloane and believed the anguish and panic on her face.

Chapter Twenty-nine

Sloane told me everything Mrs. Braverman said, which wasn't much. She said there had been instances where she could hear Nick communicating with the demon, and they definitely wanted the blame for Clara's failure to transfer placed on my father.

"I don't understand why Nick would want that. They've been best friends for years." I'd been wading through the murky confusion of deceit and false stories for months now and was frazzled from the struggle of trying to make sense of pieces that seemed not to go together.

"I don't know. Power, maybe? Nick is your father's right hand. If it looks like Nathan is messing things up for priors, or worse, is corrupt, then eventually he'll be pushed out of AfterCorps, won't he? And Nick will be in charge."

"We have to warn my parents," I said.

"I agree. But the first thing we need to do is get Clara transferred. Once she goes, the demon will probably find another weak prior to inhabit, but it will buy us a little time to get your dad involved, and he can take the lead on this."

I couldn't let myself be paralyzed by the guilt I felt at letting myself be manipulated into believing my dad was behind something sinister. I'd been told so many partial truths and half lies that it was no wonder I'd lost faith in people I'd trusted in the past. Sloane was right; our best shot was to help Clara transfer so that the worst of all this would be thwarted, at least for a little while. Long enough that my dad could figure out what to do about Nick.

We'd spent the rest of the night reading through the textbooks, learning what we needed to do in order to get Clara's transfer done. Somewhere near two o'clock in the morning, I noticed Sloane starting to fall asleep. I watched her eyelids slide down and her mouth open slightly. I couldn't imagine what I'd do without her and didn't want to. My heart filled with love and gratitude that she was here with me, ready to go to hell and back. I curled myself into the space beside her, and not long after that, I drifted off too.

❖

"Today's the day," Sloane said softly the next morning. "Are you ready?"

"I'm ready for tonight," I whispered back. "I'm dreading hanging around with Nick, acting like everything is normal."

"Me too. I'm planning to avoid him as much as possible."

I frowned. "That's not a good idea. I mean, I don't want to spend time with him either, but we have to pretend everything is normal. It's just one day, right?"

"Yeah, you're right." Part of me wondered if we really should put our plan into action. What if Sloane was wrong? But I knew she wasn't. I hadn't forgotten the look on her face when she'd come back last night. My biggest concern was that we weren't well equipped to take on a demon, but we couldn't afford to wait. We didn't have experience or power on our side; the only thing we had was the element of surprise. We needed to get this done before Nick realized something was off.

We took turns showering and went to the living room together. Nick sat at the kitchen table eating a salad and watching the news.

"Hey, sleepyheads!" he said when he saw us. "I thought about coming in to wake you, but I figured if you were still sleeping, you really needed it. There's coffee if you want some."

"Thanks." I nudged Sloane toward the coffeepot, and she filled two large mugs while I got the buttered praline creamer from the fridge.

"Are you hungry?" he asked. "I made enough salad to share, and there's chicken breast in the fridge if you want to cook some."

"I think I'm okay with coffee for now," I said. "Thank you, though."

"Yeah, thanks," Sloane said.

"Okay. Well, it's there when you're ready." He glanced at his phone. "Listen, I have some business to take care of, so I'll be in my bedroom most of the day. Answering emails, on and off conference calls. This investigation into Nathan's work practices has gotten rolling pretty quickly the last few days, and all of a sudden, I'm bogged down. You two know how to make yourselves at home, so just keep doing that."

"Sure, sounds good." I was careful to keep the contempt out of my voice. Nick had been my friend; he'd been my father's *best* friend. It was hard to reconcile that with this monster who sent a demon after me and wanted my dad to take the fall.

"Good. You know where to find me if you need anything."

"Yeah, we know where you are," Sloane said. I tapped her foot under the table when I heard the sharpness in her voice. "Thanks for everything, Nick."

"Hey, no problem. You guys are my responsibility, after all." He grabbed his water bottle and phone, and after putting his dishes in the dishwasher, walked down the hall. Sloane and I stayed silent until we heard his bedroom door close.

"So, I guess we lucked out?" I said. "We didn't want to hang out with him, and he doesn't have the time to spend with us."

"I guess so. I'll be glad when we can put tonight behind us."

I craved safety and normalcy now. If tonight went the way we hoped, it could be the beginning of getting a little bit of those back again. If it didn't…I couldn't even imagine the consequences.

❖

We got through the rest of the day with only briefly seeing Nick. Sloane and I had put together the ingredients for a vegetarian chili the previous day and turned on the slow cooker. Nick was finishing his second bowl of chili when we came out to the kitchen to get our own. We ate quietly, our minds on the task at hand tonight.

We decided to wait until after midnight to leave for AfterCorps, hopefully ensuring that Nick would be asleep. Around eleven, we began our preparations. Sloane let me borrow a pair of black jeans to go with my lightweight long-sleeved black T-shirt. I pulled my hair into a high bun, and Sloane covered her much lighter hair with a dark beanie.

We'd ripped the pages regarding final transfers from the textbooks in case we needed them for reference. Several pages were covered in marks from our pens and highlighters. We put the pages in the backpack between the mace and the flashlights, along with the other supplies.

"Did you tell Clara what time we'd be meeting her?" My heart clenched when I realized our plan could easily fail if Clara didn't know where to be and when.

"No, I don't think she has a sense of time. She said she'd be there. I don't think she had any intentions of leaving AfterCorps."

"Unless the demon makes her."

Sloane took my hands. "This is our best chance, Aria. We have to do this. No matter how things go tonight, when we leave AfterCorps, we will go to your parents' house for help. But we can set your dad up for a huge advantage if we can make this happen." We'd briefly considered telling my dad; Sloane had even left it up to me, but I'd been through too much with the people in my life to truly trust anyone with this besides Sloane.

"Okay," I said. "You're right." I checked the time. Five after midnight. I listened for any sign that Nick was awake, but the house was silent. "I guess it's time."

Sloane nodded. She put the backpack on, and I followed her out the sliding glass door.

❖

We entered the rear doors and stood inside for a few moments, much the way we'd stood at Nick's before we left, evaluating any noises for signs of someone else in the building. There was nothing.

We crept through the hallway and down the basement stairs, pausing at the bottom to let our eyes adjust. We'd agreed not to use our flashlights until we were just outside the transfer room. We let our memory of the space guide us to the elevator that took us to the clerk's department, the walkway toward the marble area outside the judiciary room, and the echoing hall leading to the smaller elevator that went down to final transfers.

I clasped Sloane's hand on the final elevator. I hadn't remembered it being so small or feeling so claustrophobic last time, and there had been three of us.

"Slow your breathing," she whispered.

I squeezed her hand and inhaled deeply, held the breath for several seconds, and exhaled as slowly as I was able. I took another breath, and when I finished, the elevator doors opened.

I unzipped the backpack on Sloane's back and got our flashlights. As we walked toward the transfer area, I was reminded that we didn't really need the light. The blazing, blinding light in the transfer alcove filled the room more fully than I remembered. The glow reached even as far back as we were as our footsteps reverberated across the cavernous room.

I'd been keeping an eye out for Clara, and I knew by the way Sloane's neck craned that she was looking too. There'd been no sign, but I noticed movement in the depths of the transfer room, and I turned. When I saw who it was, I jumped.

"Edgar?" Sloane said.

"Who is it?" The words mirrored the ones he'd said the first time we came here.

"Uh, it's Sloane…Dennison. And Aria Jasper."

The old man nodded slowly. "I've been expecting you."

"You have?" I stepped a bit closer.

"Careful," he said. "This light isn't meant for your eyes. Avert them for your safety."

"What are you doing here so late?" I asked. "And what do you mean you've been expecting us?"

"I am here because I am always here."

"You mean…you live here?" Sloane asked.

Edgar smiled. "I exist here. I do not live anywhere."

"You're a prior?"

"Of sorts. When I died, I was chosen for the honor of Chief Officer of Transfers. I get to hold the hands of my deceased brethren as they become alive again. Most fulfilling, more than makes up for giving up my earthly sight."

I wanted to ask him what that meant, why he had to give up his sight, but Clara appeared beside him.

"Is it time, Edgar?" She glanced around the room. "I don't have much time. I just barely got away."

"Yes, we shall do it now." He turned to Sloane and me. "We must form a circle around Clara. Careful of the light, young ones; it is not meant for you."

Sloane and I stepped forward, each taking one of Edgar's hands. Clara stood in the middle.

"Bow," Edgar said. The three of us bent at the waist before Clara, and she bowed as well, touching the top of her head to the top of Edgar's. "Close your eyes!"

I closed my eyes and felt as if I might be blinded by the beaming light that became so intense, it felt as if it was trying to find its way inside my eyelids and scorch my corneas.

"Go now, Clara," Edgar said. "Go now, with the heartache of the earth behind you and the peace of the new world ahead."

The room went from blazing to pitch. I opened my eyes, trying to see if Clara still stood in the center of the ring, but all I saw was darkness. If I hadn't been holding the hands of Edgar and Sloane, I would've been scared I was alone.

"Is she gone?" I couldn't tell for sure, but it seemed like the alcove was beginning to glow again. It was very faint, like when the night sky first starts to move toward the morning, but it was happening. Seconds later, I began to be able to make out the vague outlines of Sloane and Edgar.

"Oh, she's gone," a voice behind me said. "And just what am I going to do with the three of you?"

I turned. I recognized that voice. I'd known it my whole life: Nick.

Slow footsteps clapped across the floor. Sloane and I had been careful to wear soft-soled shoes so as not to make a lot of noise when we walked, but Nick had taken no such precautions.

Sloane found my hand and held tightly. I sensed Edgar behind us, but I didn't want to look to see where he was or what he was doing. I stared in front of me, eyes aching from the strain of trying to find Nick in the dark.

"You two snuck out of the house, broke into both Jasper Funeral Home *and* AfterCorps and transferred a prior I'd been keeping here for weeks." He paused. He'd stopped walking toward us, and his voice bounced off every surface, making it hard to determine where he was. I realized we were at a further disadvantage because we stood in front of the very softly glowing alcove, backlit, and Nick might have a fairly good view of us.

"The only good part about this is that you've freed a very powerful demon in the process."

I dropped Sloane's hand and moved closer to her in what I hoped looked like a cowering movement. I reached to her back and slowly, as quietly as possible, began to unzip the back flap where we'd put the mace. Every move of the zipper sounded thunderous in my ears, and I hoped that wherever Nick was, he didn't see or hear what I was doing.

"I guess I can thank you for that," he said, his voice quieter and with a sinister shade, "but maybe I'll let the demon itself thank you."

I got the flap open wide enough that I could stick my hand inside. I searched clumsily. I felt through what seemed like an entire book's worth of papers. I dug deeper.

"It won't be the first time a demon and I took care of someone in your family, Aria, but it's been a long time. Not since your grandfather have I had the pleasure." I froze for a second at this revelation. Nick had been responsible for my grandfather's death, and what was more, he was confident enough that Sloane and I would meet a similar fate that he was confessing.

My fingers closed around the mace. I pulled it out and held it behind Sloane's back, slipping my index finger under the safety latch and resting it on the trigger button.

"It's a travesty, you know. My lineage has some of the most gifted interpreters in the history of AfterCorps, but we've always come in second because you can't beat a Jasper at a Jasper's game. Except, of course, I have. Your grandfather had to meet a tragic end, and a poetically similar tragedy will strike you. I probably won't even have to continue my investigation into your father's corruption. He'll be so devastated at your loss, he'll probably hand AfterCorps to me and get as far away from all of this as he can."

The light in the alcove, grew bright enough that I could see the outline of his large frame. He had been edging around the wall to the right, and now he stepped away from it.

"And you, Sloane. You're going to die a hero, trying to defend your love. I'll make you a legend."

I saw the knife shimmering in his hand. It felt like time was moving rapidly but also in slow motion. I bumped Sloane out of the way and charged, stretching out my arm and pointing the mace.

Great pain invaded my body. I was colder than I'd ever been, and a sharp, agonizing ache started at the nape of my neck and went up into my head, then down my spine and into my arms and legs. I lost control, and as I slipped to the floor, my limbs contorted. The mace sprayed all around me, and earthy, spicy fumes filled the air. Even as I writhed, I started coughing, and I heard Sloane and Nick choking. Nick. Was he still holding the knife? Where was Sloane? I struggled to stay conscious. The world was fading to black, and I heard Edgar speaking in a language I didn't recognize.

Inch by inch, vertebra by vertebra, the freezing pain began to lift. I lay on the floor, coughing and rasping, but otherwise feeling a relief course through my body that only came after extreme misery.

My vision was starting to come back after the dark gray haze, and I could hear Edgar. His voice, which had been so soothing and gentle, was a rumbling storm that clashed across the open chamber.

"Perhaps you've forgotten that I was in the CDU with Aria's grandfather long before you came along. He was a good man."

I stared through the fog and saw Nick on the floor. He was coughing, but he was also twisting in anguish and looked a lot like a snake slithering across the ground.

Edgar rested a hand on the back of my neck. The dull ache that had replaced the stabbing cold pain subsided. "Can you stand?" he asked. I got to my feet, a little wobbly and unsure but standing nonetheless. I looked for Sloane and saw her curled in a ball on the floor, still coughing.

An inky shadow filled the room, towering over us. A rotten smell permeated my nostrils, and at first I thought it was the remnants of mace. The cold became so thick that it felt as if the lining of my lungs was crystalizing when I inhaled.

"The demon." Edgar's voice was hoarse. "Aria, you must banish it."

I rushed to the backpack grabbed the pages. With shaking hands, I shuffled through the thin papers until I found the one I needed. Before I could begin to speak, I made the mistake of looking at the demon, and its magnitude distracted me. The shadow loomed and expanded, swallowing its surroundings in darkness. I couldn't see a face, body, or any features; it was simply a shadowy nothingness eating at the transfer room. My hair fluttered around my face as a freezing gust of air shot across the room. A second blast hit my body before I could catch my breath, this one even colder than the last, and then the chamber became a wind tunnel, and I tumbled into Edgar.

"Hurry, child," he croaked.

Sloane appeared at my side and held the other end of the pages. We extended our hands into the air and made fists. Our voice raised above the wind as the shadow pooled closer and closer to us:

> *Life's blood,*
> *Death's decree,*
> *Demon, from you,*
> *We are free,*
> *Your name is Darkness,*
> *It is your claim,*
> *You now go back from whence you came.*

The wind howled and shrieked, and for a moment, I heard my name screamed at a deafeningly high pitch. The darkness had continued to spread, and even as we recited our words, Sloane and I had backed into a corner, shuffling Edgar along with us. The entire room had been swallowed, all except for a rectangular portion the size of a Volkswagen van.

Slowly at first, the shadow began to reverse. Inch by inch, the transfer chamber reappeared, but as it did, the wind raged more violently. It jerked me from my space between Sloane and Edgar, and freezing tendrils like long, icy fingers gripped my right arm and dragged across the slick, shiny floor toward the disappearing darkness. I reached out frantically, trying to grab anything, but there was nothing to hold on to.

"No!" Sloane ran to me, and we locked our arms around each other. Terrified, I caught a glimpse of her eyes and saw gritty determination in them. I took a deep breath, and the two of us began to heave ourselves toward Edgar and the safety in the corner.

"Step!" I had to yell so she could hear me above the screaming gale. We sidestepped together and paused to gather our strength, then repeated. Edgar had his hands out, and after minutes that seemed like hours, we were able to grasp them. Sloane and I collapsed onto the floor together, out of breath and worn out.

The wind stopped. It was so abrupt that one moment we felt as if we'd been sucked up inside a tornado and the next everything went still and silent, with not even a whisper of what we'd endured. The room was empty and as serene as it had been the first time we'd visited with Nick, which reminded me:

"Where's Nick?"

"He…he got pulled into the darkness, I think," Sloane said. "It covered everything, and now he's gone."

"You're right," Edgar said. "He was folded into the shadows."

I had no love for Nick anymore, but getting swallowed up by a demon seemed a terrible ending, even for him. "What'll happen to him? What will the demon do?"

"I'm not entirely sure, but demons tend not to play nicely, especially with those who summon them as pawns in earthly games."

I thought about Nick and the terrible punishment he faced. After everything he'd put my family through, I couldn't bring myself to feel sorry for him. I regretted that someone we had loved and trusted had turned out to be such a poisonous, destructive, and evil presence in our lives. He had wanted to destroy us, and he'd almost succeeded. An eternity spent with a demon wasn't something I'd wish on anyone, but I was glad he was gone.

Epilogue

I like your new digs!" Sloane had taken the two-minute tour of my studio apartment in Hungarian Village, a neighborhood made mostly of row houses just south of downtown.

"Thanks. It's nothing fancy, but it'll do for now." I crossed the room to the kitchen counter where she was putting some plates into the cupboard for me. I linked my arms around her waist. "And it gives us plenty of space to be alone."

She turned to face me. "Even better." She leaned down and kissed me.

"What do you want for dinner?" I walked back over to some boxes in the corner and started unpacking. "I haven't bought groceries yet, but I can spring for delivery when you get hungry."

"How about Chinese? There's that great place a few blocks away. We can even walk over and pick it up if you want to get some air."

"Sounds great."

I pulled a few books out of the box and arranged them on my bookshelf. When I bent back down, I saw the training manual from Nick's class, and the paper sticking out of it had his handwriting on it. It was the exercise he'd asked us to do where we discussed AfterCorps and what it meant to us. I sat on the floor and looked at his jagged letters, not reading but letting my eyes pass over them.

It had been a couple of months since Sloane and I vanquished the demon, sending Nick with it. My father had performed an investigation and found a small faction of AfterCorps workers who had helped Nick with his plans to frame my father for keeping priors earthbound. Power had been what he'd been after all along.

I missed the Nick who'd been present my whole life, and I knew my dad both missed and mourned the man he'd considered a brother. All of us—Mom, Dad, Sloane, and I—we all suffered from the trauma we'd endured at his hands, and it was very difficult to reconcile that monster with the man we'd loved and admired.

We'd found out a lot about Nick during those weeks. He'd been responsible for keeping Clara and many other priors earthbound in an attempt to frame my dad. He'd been the one who'd released me, and later, Sloane, making us vulnerable to the demon's attacks. My dad and Edgar held a small ceremony, putting us back under protection so we wouldn't have to communicate with priors unless we were under the watchful eyes of someone experienced enough to handle them.

I filled my time doing as much singing as possible. I was becoming acclimated to the death singer biz and was also taking the occasional gigs around town. Weddings, mostly, and the irony of that wasn't lost on me, but I was making enough money to have my own place, and after months of feeling suffocated by the traps and responsibilities of my new life, it was what I really needed.

"You okay?" Sloane came over to see what I was doing, and I heard her breath catch when she saw what I was looking at. She sat beside me and rested her hand on my knee. "Still hard to believe, isn't it?"

I nodded. We'd had several weeks' break before they found an interim instructor to continue classes for Sloane and me until the board could reach a decision on who the permanent replacement should be. It had been difficult to even step back into our training room, but we'd done it. Our first day back, we walked into the room, hand in hand, ready to face whatever came next together.

"You know, I think I'm ready for that walk now," I said. "You wanna go see if that Chinese place is as good as you've heard?"

"Sure."

We stood, dusted our backsides off, and headed out the door. In the hallway outside my apartment, there was a garbage chute door, and I stuffed the paper with Nick's handwriting into it before stepping outside into the bright September sun.

About the Author

Nan Higgins wrote her first book—a seven-page ghost story about the rickety old Victorian farmhouse she grew up in—when she was ten, and she has been writing ever since. She majored in music theater and puts her schooling to use by singing and dancing much more often than her friends and family think necessary. She is the cohost of *Stalled*, a podcast about the victories and struggles of two writers who got a late start trying to turn their passions into their profession. She is also the creator and host of the new podcast *A Gay with Words*, in which she explores the labels and language used in the queer community.

Books Available From Bold Strokes Books

Face the Music by Ali Vali. Sweet music is the last thing that happens when Nashville music producer Mason Liner and daughter of country royalty Victoria Roddy are thrown together in an effort to save country star Sophie Roddy's career. (978-1-63555-532-5)

Flavor of the Month by Georgia Beers. What happens when baker Charlie and chef Emma realize their differing paths have led them right back to each other? (978-1-63555-616-2)

Mending Fences by Angie Williams. Rancher Bobbie Del Rey and veterinarian Grace Hammond are about to discover if heartbreaks of the past can ever truly be mended. (978-1-63555-708-4)

Silk and Leather: Lesbian Erotica with an Edge, edited by Victoria Villaseñor. This collection of stories by award-winning authors offers fantasies as soft as silk and tough as leather. The only question is: How far will you go to make your deepest desires come true? (978-1-63555-587-5)

The Last Place You Look by Aurora Rey. Dumped by her wife and looking for anything but love, Julia Pierce retreats to her hometown only to rediscover high school friend Taylor Winslow, who's secretly crushed on her for years. (978-1-63555-574-5)

The Mortician's Daughter by Nan Higgins. A singer on the verge of stardom discovers she must give up her dreams to live a life in service to ghosts. (978-1-63555-594-3)

The Real Thing by Laney Webber. When passion flares between actress Virginia Green and masseuse Allison McDonald, can they be sure it's the real thing? (978-1-63555-478-6)

What the Heart Remembers Most by M. Ullrich. For college sweethearts Jax Levine and Gretchen Mills, could an accident be the second chance neither knew they wanted? (978-1-63555-401-4)

White Horse Point by Andrews & Austin. Mystery writer Taylor James finds herself falling for the mysterious woman on White Horse Point who lives alone, protecting a secret she can't share about a murderer who walks among them. (978-1-63555-695-7)

Femme Tales by Anne Shade. Six women find themselves in their own real-life fairy tales when true love finds them in the most unexpected ways. (978-1-63555-657-5)

Jellicle Girl by Stevie Mikayne. One dark summer night, Beth and Jackie go out to the canoe dock. Two years later, Beth is still carrying the weight of what happened to Jackie. (978-1-63555-691-9)

My Date with a Wendigo by Genevieve McCluer. Elizabeth Rosseau finds her long-lost love and the secret community of fiends she's now a part of. (978-1-63555-679-7)

On the Run by Charlotte Greene. Even when they're cute blondes, it's stupid to pick up hitchhikers, especially when they've just broken out of prison, but doing so is about to change Gwen's life forever. (978-1-63555-682-7)

Perfect Timing by Dena Blake. The choice between love and family has never been so difficult, and Lynn's and Maggie's different visions of the future may end their romance before it's begun. (978-1-63555-466-3)

The Mail Order Bride by R. Kent. When a mail order bride is thrust on Austin, he must choose between the bride he never wanted or the dream he lives for. (978-1-63555-678-0)

Through Love's Eyes by C.A. Popovich. When fate reunites Brittany Yardin and Amy Jansons, can they move beyond the pain of their past to find love? (978-1-63555-629-2)

To the Moon and Back by Melissa Brayden. Film actress Carly Daniel thinks that stage work is boring and unexciting, but when she accepts a lead role in a new play, stage manager Lauren Prescott tests both her heart and her ability to share the limelight. (978-1-63555-618-6)

Tokyo Love by Diana Jean. When Kathleen Schmitt is given the opportunity to be on the cutting edge of AI technology, she never thought a failed robotic love companion would bring her closer to her neighbor, Yuriko Velucci, and finding love in unexpected places. (978-1-63555-681-0)

Brooklyn Summer by Maggie Cummings. When opposites attract, can a summer of passion and adventure lead to a lifetime of love? (978-1-63555-578-3)

City Kitty and Country Mouse by Alyssa Linn Palmer. Pulled in two different directions, can a city kitty and a country mouse fall in love and make it work? (978-1-63555-553-0)

Elimination by Jackie D. When a dangerous homegrown terrorist seeks refuge with the Russian mafia, the team will be put to the ultimate test. (978-1-63555-570-7)

In the Shadow of Darkness by Nicole Stiling. Angeline Vallencourt is a reluctant vampire who must decide what she wants more—obscurity, revenge, or the woman who makes her feel alive. (978-1-63555-624-7)

On Second Thought by C. Spencer. Madisen is falling hard for Rae. Even single life and co-parenting are beginning to click. At least, that is, until her ex-wife begins to have second thoughts. (978-1-63555-415-1)

Out of Practice by Carsen Taite. When attorney Abby Keane discovers the wedding blogger tormenting her client is the woman she had a passionate, anonymous vacation fling with, sparks and subpoenas fly. Legal Affairs: one law firm, three best friends, three chances to fall in love. (978-1-63555-359-8)

Providence by Leigh Hays. With every click of the shutter, photographer Rebekiah Kearns finds it harder and harder to keep Lindsey Blackwell in focus without getting too close. (978-1-63555-620-9)

Taking a Shot at Love by KC Richardson. When academic and athletic worlds collide, will English professor Celeste Bouchard and basketball coach Lisa Tobias ignore their attraction to achieve their professional goals? (978-1-63555-549-3)

Flight to the Horizon by Julie Tizard. Airline captain Kerri Sullivan and flight attendant Janine Case struggle to survive an emergency water landing and overcome dark secrets to give love a chance to fly. (978-1-63555-331-4)